JERRY felt a searing pain in his side as Nick aimed his gun and, covering Jerry's body with his own, fired rapidly. The figure in the ragged German uniform dropped from sight.

RICK read through the names on the monument once again. He stood at attention, taps playing silently in his head, as one face after another floated gently by. Wiping his eyes, he went to join the others.

IVY had had cosmetic surgery once too often. The skin on her face was pulled grotesquely tight. "Does she know about her husband and grandson?" "She knows what she wants to know. In her heart she'll always be the homecoming queen."

SOPHIE wept silently. If only she hadn't frozen and hung up the phone. If only she had not gone to that dance. If only she had been honest with Stefan when he first returned. So many "if onlys."

JOE pulled a well-worn picture of a Spanish galleon from a drawer near the beautifully carved model, "This is the one Miss Freeman told me I should build. I been workin' on it for a few years now. I hope I get to finish it."

DAISY sobbed, "I can't believe it. We've been married for fifty years and I didn't know. I've hated my mother for what she made that doctor do to me. Now I thank God I didn't have kids for him to destroy."

Additional Works by E.R. Turner

The Reunion; From 1915 to 1997 generations of Marsh family members learn to cope with and learn from the events and times in which they live.

To Seek a Bird's Nest; Four generations of Elizabeths, from the 1890s to the 1990s, work to deal with challenges specific to their individual situations.

Beware the Nothing Much; Emma must decide whether her decision will cause an innocent man to be condemned or bring peril to her own life.

Trapped in the Uintas; Rebecca and Doug know there are wild animals in the Uinta Mountains but, while on their vacation trip there, find their lives threatened by a two-legged predator.

Crimson-Laced Sunsets; One life, from joy to heartache to contentment told in verse.

The Class of '44

by
E.R. Turner

Copyright © 1999 by Ella Ruth Bergera

ALL RIGHTS RESERVED.
No part of this book may be reproduced in any form whatsoever, whether by graphic, visual, electronic, filming, microfilming, tape recording, or any other means, without written permission of the author, except in the case of brief passages embodied in critical reviews and articles where the ISBN and author are mentioned.

This book is a work of fiction. Characters in this story are the work of the author's imagination and any resemblance to real people is coincidental.

Distributed by:
Granite Publishing and Distribution, L.L.C.
2868 North 1430 West • Orem, Utah 84057
(801) 229-9023 • Toll Free (800) 574-5779
FAX (801) 229-1924

ISBN: 1-57636-078-4
Library of Congress Catalog Card Number: 99-66686
Production by: *SunRise Publishing, Orem, Utah*

Wickedness never works
Mosiah
concerns
good honest individuals
(room affect if you
don't by
accept
Book and the
wicked

Alma - Nehor had
Gideon man of God
was killed by
Nehor - who preached
false doctrine

Tide feely
the gospel by
the spirit —
awake up call
for me.
impact — the
resonates the
humble view
it from God
(Tithe) don't worry
principles — faithful
the challenges

Across the fields of yesterday
    He sometimes comes to me,
A little lad just back from play,
    The lad I used to be.

And, yet, he smiles so wistfully
    Once he has crept within.
I wonder if he hopes to see
    The man I might have been.

                    —*T.S. Jones Jr.*

Chapter One

The strains of *Stardust* wafted gently through the night air as Jerry and Emma walked into the room. A large gold-embossed 50 with smaller blue numbers, 1944-1994, was positioned above the bandstand. On closer look they could see the resemblance of some of the orchestra members to the Harry Gould Band members who had played at their high school dances.

"Looks like a younger version of the guys we knew," Jerry smiled. "Must be some of their kids and grandkids."

"Yes. And look, they've even decorated the place exactly like it looked at our graduation dance."

Emma fitted comfortably in Jerry's arms as they joined the dancers already in motion, swaying slowly to the music.

"I think I'm glad we came, after all."

"Yeah. Me too."

They had been on tour in Europe during the 25th year anniversary reunion and had been undecided about attending this year. Neither one were big on class reunions. But, in the past year they had come face to face with their own mortality and realized that they did, after all, want to join this celebration with their former classmates.

Glancing around they recognized friends from both their Grassville days and their Sommerset High School years. Some of them took longer to place than others, then a smile or a laugh or a tilt of head brought them into focus.

Without stopping, the orchestra moved smoothly into *Deep Purple*. Emma closed her eyes as she leaned her head on Jerry's shoulder, remembering dancing to these songs years ago. They didn't go dancing anymore. Somewhere along the way of raising children and welcoming grandchildren they had kept busy doing other things.

"I didn't realize how much I missed doing this."

Jerry smiled. She had always loved to dance. "Remember the first time I asked you to dance?"

"How could I forget. I was so unsure of myself and trying to cover it up with braggadocio. I'm still surprised you ever asked me again."

He lifted her chin and looked deep into her loving, hazel eyes. "I knew it was show." He gently brushed her lips with his. "I figured if I was patient you'd finally come to know how special you were."

"Well, you knew more than I did."

They moved easily as the music shifted to *Moonglow* and then *Whispering*. Music like this had been so much a part of their life all those years ago. Years that had gone faster than either of them realized. Until six months ago.

"Will you say anything to anyone?"

"No. I want to enjoy tonight. I want to go back for awhile and live those years again. Those simple, uncomplicated years."

"They weren't all uncomplicated," Jerry said quietly.

"I know. But tonight I just want to remember the good times. I don't want to think about 'the nothing much,' or being 'neither cold nor hot.' I want to melt into this music and capture one moment of my youth." She grinned ruefully, "I'm not making much sense, am I?"

"You're making plenty of sense." Jerry's arms tightened around her, "And I agree. Let's go with the flow, as Becca would say, and step back in time...at least for tonight."

~ ~ ~

"Hey, you two, glad you could make it. Long time no see."

They turned to see Billy Hoffstein heading toward them. Bill, not Billy, Emma had to remind herself.

"Good to see you, too," Jerry said in surprise as they shook hands, "Last we heard you were teaching overseas."

"Right. Just got back last month." He smiled, "And as much as I liked it, it's really good to be back in this country. Russia is still struggling economically and politically."

"Did Sylvia go with you?"

"She did the first year but when Arlys was expecting our first grandchild, she wanted to be there to help, so she came back last fall." He glanced around the crowded room "She's here somewhere. I know she'll want to see you. Oh, here she comes now."

They watched as a smiling, delicate-boned woman walked toward them. "Just look at you, Emma Harris. You haven't aged a day!"

"Oh please," Emma grimaced, "I hope I didn't look this old the last time we saw you."

The two couples laughed as they walked to a table piled with mounds of fresh fruit and desserts of every kind. They filled their plates and moved over to an empty table.

"Tell us about your family. Where are they now? And are you still living in Salt Lake?"

"Yes," Jerry answered. "And our kids live fairly close by."

"Becky and her family live in Provo, although her daughter, Becca, is in Salt Lake now teaching school." Emma said, "Nicco and his family live in Springville. His oldest son is getting married next month."

Jerry continued, "Emily and her husband live in Logan. They both teach at the university there. And Tommy is the golf pro in Nephi. But enough about us. Tell us about your family."

"As I said, Arlys presented us with our first grandchild in December," Bill said proudly. A shadow flickered across his face, "And Joseph is still trying to find himself."

"He will," Sylvia said quietly. "We married late, too."

This was obviously a prickly subject. "Tell us about your brother, Joe," Emma said. "We heard he's not well."

"He's not," Bill said sadly. "When Sally died he just seemed to give up. I don't think any of us realized how much they meant to each other."

At Mrs. Hoffstein's death when Joe was ten years old and Billy had just turned three, taking over the care of the house and his little brother fell to Joe. Their father was a good, hardworking man who left for work early in the morning and returned ten or twelve hours later. Neighbors pitched in to help but the main responsibility was left to Joe.

He was excellent at working with his hands, kept the house clean and simple meals on the table. He was retained in school often enough that when he finished seventh grade and turned eighteen he stopped trying to succeed in school and followed in his father's footsteps who had left school at age thirteen.

By this time Joe was working part time at the sawmill in town and when school was out that year Mr. Kenner gave him a full time job there. His success there was no surprise to those who knew him well.

Billy, on the other hand, was bright and talented, skipping grades until, though he was two years younger than Emma and Jerry, he graduated from high school with them. He received a full scholarship to the University of Utah and from there went on to graduate school at Berkeley then to Yale where he graduated at the top of his class.

He met Sylvia Landa at Yale where she was working for her degree in law. They were married in their late thirties and produced two children a few years later. Although they were brilliant and successful, they stayed close to Billy's father and brother, returning home to visit as often as possible.

On a visit home during the late 1960s Bill and Joe walked slowly through the old cemetery. "Will you stay here now with dad gone?"

"Yeah."

"You're more than welcome to come and live with us."

"I know that, Billy, and I appreciate it. But this is my home."

"Yes. I told Sylvia that. But she wanted me to be sure you understand she would welcome you."

"She's a good woman. I'm glad you found each other. Even though," Joe laughed, "sometimes dad and me wondered if you'd ever find the need for a woman. You always seemed to be too busy learnin' and teachin' and travelin'."

Bill smiled, "To tell the truth, until I met Sylvia I didn't realize I was missing out on something. My work was always everything I ever needed. But after I met her I realized it wasn't enough. My life wasn't complete. I was really lucky to find her...and that she'd have me."

Bill's eyes were filled with compassion as he looked at this older brother who had given so much, who had always been such a rock for him and for their dad. What would happen to him now? That he could take care of himself was not a problem. Joe had been doing that all his life. But he hated the thought of him coming home to an empty house day after day. Everybody needs someone, he thought wryly, remembering just how long it took him to learn that.

Joe's eyes lit up and a broad smile spread across his face"

"It's okay, Billy. I got somethin' to tell you."

* * *

Easter weekend in 1969 Jerry and Emma took their children home to Grassville. Jerry's relatives had moved to Logan by this time but Emma's parents, Olivia and Tom Williams, still lived in the little house in which Emma had grown up. Everyone in the family had encouraged them to move to a bigger house but they had said there was no reason to; this house had all the room they needed now.

And it was true. Tom had remodeled it adding a modern bathroom and Olivia had decorated the house in soft creams and blues. They had sold some of their property to families from southern California looking to relocate in a small town away from the increasing smog and rising crime in that area. The slow pace appealed to retirees from Salt Lake and Ogden, too, and by this time Grassville was taking on a new look.

A nine hole golf course was built where 'tag town' had once existed and a drug store now stood where the confectionary had been. The store was now a supermarket and an indoor swimming pool had been erected adjacent to the tennis court. The sawmill was still in operation supplying lumber to locations across Utah.

"What's ever happened to Joe Hoffstein? I know Billy is on the faculty of a university in New England but I haven't kept up much on Joe."

"He still lives here in town, Emma. Joe's the head man at the sawmill."

"You're kidding!" Emma and Jerry said in unison.

"Nope," Tom laughed, "Abe Kenner is semi-retired but he still keeps his hand in. He put Joe in as manager a couple of years ago. Word is it's in his will that Joe will get the mill when Abe passes on. His boy, Rick, never was much interested in it and when he came back after the war he told his folks he was was going to work as a forest ranger."

"How did his folks take that?"

"Fine. They knew all along the mill wasn't something he wanted to do. And last we heard Rick's doing well."

"He was their only child wasn't he? I don't remember much about him except he was quite a bit older and the first one in town to have a motorcycle." Emma glanced at Jerry, "Did you ever get to ride on it?"

"No. That must have been before I moved here. I don't remember him at all."

"Well, he was a good sport about taking us little kids for rides sometimes but that's all I remember about him." She turned to her father, "Will he mind not getting the mill?"

"I don't believe so. He's a little older than Joe and has always known him. From what I hear he's glad Joe's been there to look out for his dad and the mill all these years."

"That's great!" Jerry said. "I only really knew Joe in the seventh grade the year I moved here. He left school after that year but I remember how wood became incredibly beautiful in his hands. I'll bet he's doing a great job."

"He is." Olivia turned to Emma, "And you'll be happy to know he's getting married next month. He wanted me to be sure and tell you."

"Married? Who to?"

Tom laughed, "Guess."

Emma smiled, "I haven't a clue, but I hope it's someone who'll love and appreciate him."

"She does," Olivia replied. "She's a different person since Joe started taking an interest in her. She smiles more and doesn't seem as nervous being around people as she used to be. In fact, she glows with happiness."

"All right, already! Who is she?"

"Sally Oliver." Olivia's smile was gentle.
"Sally!? Come on. You're pulling my leg!"
"No. It's true."
"But she's awfully old for him, isn't she?"
"Actually, she is some older than him but it doesn't seem to make a bit of difference to either one of them. I've never seen them happier." Olivia paused, "She's always been childlike and when her mother died poor Sally was lost until Joe started taking her out."

"And apparently," Tom added, "he keeps an eye on her brother, too."

"What do you mean?"

"Whenever anybody sees Freddie three sheets to the wind they call Joe and he comes and takes him to his house to dry out." Tom shrugged his shoulders, "Even though Jake at *The Brewery* won't serve Freddie anymore, there are still a few jerks who think it's funny to get him drunk. But even they've tapered off since Joe started seeing Sally. Word is he's passed the word around there'll be trouble for anyone caught supplying Freddie."

"Good old Joe," Emma grinned, then began to laugh, "I think that's just wonderful. And I bet they'll be happy together. But I'll also bet Mrs. Greeley and some of her circle are having a field day about it."

"Actually, you'd be surprised," Olivia said. "Most of those women took awhile getting used to the idea but, once they did, they've been quite supportive."

"Will wonders never cease," Emma said quietly.

~ ~ ~

Tight-lipped, unsmiling Mrs. Oliver had a hard life. Her husband died of pneumonia when Freddie was five years old and Sally was two. Freddie was no ball of fire but he did get through school to graduation.

But Sally always lagged behind the children her age. It wasn't anything you could put your finger on, she just seemed to get farther behind every year.

There were no programs to help slow children and teachers didn't know how to do much with her but teach her simple reading and counting skills. By the time she had been passed from one grade to the next and was in the sixth grade she missed more days in class than she attended. Even making her stand in the hall while the whole school passed by to see what happened to sluffers didn't help.

The principal didn't know what to do either so he agreed that she would be better off at home helping her mother run her boarding house than sitting in school wasting everybody's time. At least at home she knew how to wash dishes, mop floors, hang clothes on the line and iron.

Sally's body matured early and when she reached her teens she was beautiful. Even though some of the men in town lusted after her and some of the housewives, particularly Mrs. Greeley, gossiped about her, Sally remained simple and childlike...often calling attention to herself innocently and without realizing what she was doing.

It was during this time Freddie's drinking became open and frequent. His mother tried to help him but she didn't know how. Soon he was drunk nearly all the time. He was never a mean drunk but he became the butt of jokes and snide remarks. He continued to live at home and worked as the town handyman to pay for his liquor. He forced himself to stay halfway sober long enough to finish whatever job he was hired for but spent long drunken periods between jobs.

Dealing with alcoholism and mental retardation and child or spousal abuse was completely foreign to the good citizens of Grassville. "A man's gotta do what a man's gotta do" was spoken more than once. And it was never questioned.

~ ~ ~

"Congratulations, Joe! We're so happy for you."

"Thanks. I'm so glad you could make it." He turned to the glowing woman standing beside him, "Sally, this is Emma and Jerry, came all the way from Salt Lake."

Sally smiled shyly. "I remember you, Emma. You used to sit with your friend Ivy on her porch across the street from our house when you were a kid."

"Yes, I did." But I certainly didn't realize what a beautiful woman you were, Emma thought, and still are. Mama was right, you do glow.

"I'll tell you somethin' else about Emma," Joe grinned, "She was a mighty fine tennis partner."

Emma's laugh bubbled with joy, "Don't believe a word of it. I was a lousy tennis player but Joe always made me look good when we teamed up as partners." She took their hands in hers, "I hope your future together will be wonderful."

Jerry added, "So do I. And we drove past your new house on our way over here to the church. It's a work of art."

"Thanks," Joe said shyly, "I wanted to build a home fit for Sally."

"And he added a separate apartment onto it for my brother. Freddie's not very well and we wanted him near so we can take care of him." They glanced across the room at her brother standing sober and proud in his new suit talking quietly with Mr. Kenner.

How very tactful, Emma thought. She may be re-writing history but it's obvious Sally has more on the ball than she's been given credit for. And the look on Joe's face said he was well aware of this.

"Are you going back to Salt Lake tonight?"

"No. We're staying with Emma's folks. We'll head back tomorrow."

"Well, stop in before you leave and we'll give you a tour of our place."

"Won't you be getting ready to leave on a honeymoon?"

"Nah," Joe said glancing surreptitiously at Freddie, "We decided we'll take our honeymoon right here at home."

Sally nodded contentedly.

The future looked bright for the new Mr. and Mrs. Joe Hoffstein. They accepted the reality of playing nursemaid to Freddie while still finding more joy together than either had ever dreamed possible.

* * *

"Are you staying here in Sommerset tonight?"

"No," Bill answered, "We're staying with Joe for a few days. Have you been back to Grassville lately?"

Jerry shook his head, "Not since Emma's parents died. We met there then with her family to divide up things and sell the house but we haven't been back since."

"Has it changed much?" Nostalgia tinged Emma's words, "It was such a great place to grow up."

"It's grown some but still has the same small town feel I remember." Bill pulled a newspaper clipping out of his wallet and began to unfold it.

"Where on earth did you get that?" Emma asked in surprise.

"Joe sent it to me."

"And you keep it in your wallet? Whatever for?"

Bill laughed, "I pull it out and read it when I get homesick for the old days. It expresses exactly what I remember."

Emma blushed, "I didn't think anybody would read it."

"Didn't you submit it to the *Sommerset Times*?"

"I did," Jerry grinned. "When they were doing that special county anniversary edition . . ."

"Without telling me," Emma interrupted. "I was terribly embarrassed when it came out."

"Why?"

"You've read it so you know I'm no poet. I just like to fiddle around with words."

"Well as someone once said 'I'm not an expert but I know what I like.' And I like the scenes of home that come back whenever I read this." He began to quietly read:

> Four rooms, an outhouse,
> linoleum clad floors,
> miniature closets,
> and squeaky screen doors.
> Wood from the woodpile,
> and coal from the shed
> always required
> for pies, cakes and bread.
> Kalsomined walls, varnished
> wood frames in place
> around scrubbed, spotless windows
> with curtains of lace.
> Our own mountain to climb
> with a lighthouse for play.
> Bumpy washboard-road trips
> in Dad's old Chevrolet.
> A round galvanized bathtub
> put to use Saturday night;
> then, Mother's bedtime stories filled
> with goodness and light.
> Whatever I do,
> wherever I roam,

these are the memories
I carry of home.

A pause then, "The only change I make as I read is Dad's bedtime stories. He couldn't read very well but he knew how to tell all the old tales. And whatever he couldn't remember, he improvised."

"I didn't know that about your dad."

"Nobody did. They saw him as a hard worker but never knew the creative, gentle soul Joe and I knew." Bill smiled, "Now you know why I carry this around in my wallet."

Emma shook her head, unable to say anything. The tears were too close.

Jerry stood up and pulled her to her feet. "Ready for some more dancing?"

Bill and Sylvia stood, too. "By the way, have you two seen the War Memorial for Former Sommerset High Students?"

"No. Where is it?"

"Down the hall there by the office. I was surprised by the number of kids names on it we went to school with."

"Thanks for telling us, Bill. We'll see you two again before the night's over. Come on Emma, let's go take a look."

They walked out the door and started down the hall.

E.R. Turner

Chapter Two

Jerry rubbed his fingers gently over the names carved in the marble stone.

"So many kids we went to school with," murmured Emma as she watched Jerry's serene expression masking the terrible sadness he felt. He had told her some of what the war was like but, like the others who came home after World War II, he didn't talk much about it.

As his fingers caressed the cold memorial bathed in soft light from an overhead spot, Jerry's mind was filled with the sights and sounds of carnage and destruction that had been part of his surroundings fifty years earlier as his squadron had flown bombing raids across Europe.

Jerry and his friends in their graduating class knew they would be drafted into the army as soon as they turned eighteen. So the day after graduation Jerry and Nick and Max and Robbie from Grassville, along with a half dozen of their classmates from high school, went to the recruiting office in Sommerset and joined the Army Air Corps.

Their decision was based partly on the encouraging news in the winter of that graduation year that Allied air forces combined in crushing numbers to bomb German aircraft industries. Reichsmarshal Hermann Goering, commander in chief of the proud German Luftwaffe, had boasted early in the war that Allied bombers would never reach Berlin but after those five days in February 1944, he was proven wrong.

Jerry and his friends reported to Fort Douglas in Salt Lake and were sent from there to basic training camp. When they finished their training the group was split up and sent to bases in Europe and the Pacific.

Jerry and Nick were stationed together in Italy and assigned to the same bomber squadron, part of Twining's Fifteenth Air Force. Their group joined Allied bombers in the attacks on rich oil fields in Ploiesti, Romania which finally stopped all production from that sector. In further Allied bombing raids, dams in the Ruhr Valley were destroyed depriving many German industries of their power sources.

The war caused Jerry and his buddies to grow up and take on responsibilities greater than they had ever known. They were forced to make life and death decisions instantly and the consequences of those decisions never faded from their memories.

When Jerry and Nick were transferred to a base in Sicily they fell in love with the buildings with their colorful tiled roofs and the land that was surrounded by the sparkling Mediterranean Sea. The countryside and people were entirely different from anything Jerry had ever known.

The scars of war were everywhere but the Sicilian people, impoverished but jubilant, were happy to be freed from German occupation. They welcomed the Allied troops with open arms.

His letters to Emma, who was enrolled in Brigham Young University, were filled with descriptions of the country and its people increasing her desire to travel to that part of the world some day.

After grueling days of bombing missions, the airmen were sometimes given forty-eight hour furloughs. Leaves were granted on a rotating basis so whenever Jerry and Nick both got time off duty they signed out a jeep from maintenance and drove as far into the countryside as possible.

The two visited some of the larger cities such as Catania and Palermo and Messina as well as many of the small villages dotting the island of Sicily. As they drove through the narrow, rutted village roads scores of children, hollow-eyed and gaunt ran to the edge of the road waving and calling, "Ciao, Americani!" Jerry and Nick learned early on to stock up with as many candy bars and packages of gum as they could scrounge to share with these deprived children.

There was damage everywhere from the fierce fighting that had taken place to drive the Germans out of Sicily. They learned to veer around craters and potholes and ruins skillfully, always on the alert for new hazards.

Nick's parents had emigrated from Italy before he was born so he was fluent in the language, although the dialect varied somewhat from the pronunciations he had learned at home. And Jerry quickly picked up Italian words and phrases as he listened to Nick converse with the Italian people they encountered on these journeys.

When they visited Monreale they were invited to join a wedding procession which wound from the Duomo to the main square where everyone had brought something from their meager store of food to share with the wedding party. When it was time to get back in the jeep and head back to the base, both young men were tired but delighted with this touch of normality in a world gone mad.

In the ancient village of Gratteri they found the people warm and friendly and wanting to know about America and these young men who were so far from home. They asked about their parents and families and thanked them for coming to free them from Nazi rule. The people talked solemnly about the fall from power of Mussolini and their delight when premier Badoglio's government signed the armistice with the Allies the previous year. But it was their trip into Mistretta which changed everything for them.

~ ~ ~

As the jeep slowly climbed the winding road into the heart of Mistretta, Jerry said, "Back when we were growing up, did you ever dream you'd see this part of the world?"

"Naw," Nick laughed, "my parents talked about taking me to the old country for a visit some day but in those days a trip to Sommerset was enough of a highlight for me. What about you? Did you expect to travel?"

"I wanted to."

"You did? How come you never said anything?"

Jerry laughed, "Are you kidding. I was already considered a misfit when I arrived in Grassville. If I'd said a word about wanting to travel I'd have been run out of town."

Nick nodded, remembering how Jerry had been treated by the kids in Grassville when he arrived there the summer between sixth and seventh grades. Rumors spread rapidly that Jerry had been taken from his parents...or they had kicked him out. Whatever the case, Jerry lived with his aunt and uncle, Jim and Emily Harris.

Right from the beginning he had been different than the other kids in town. He kept to himself and didn't join in their games at the tennis court or the swimming pool they had built in the creek above town. Kids called him names behind his back and mocked him to his face.

Nick hadn't really got to know him until their seventh grade English class. It was obvious from the start of the year that the kids in Miss Freeman's class were good at and liked reading. Until she came to teach most of them had kept their love of books to themselves. Reading wasn't a high priority and some of the bullies their age made it hard on any kids caught reading for fun.

But even in that class Jerry never volunteered answers or called attention to himself. Until their last English class the day before school was out.

That day Miss Freeman had them read together a poem about the importance of making choices. They struggled to make sense of the main theme of the poem, wandering around the core of the issue until Jerry, for the first time, raised his hand and made the meaning clear to all of them. With that, his acceptance as one of them grew.

By the time they entered the larger world of high school in Sommerset where all the kids in the surrounding small towns were bussed, Nick and Jerry had several classes together and often compared homework on their way to and from school. It was at these times Nick came to know the depth and intelligence Jerry possessed.

Jerry never talked about his childhood or his reason for living with his aunt and uncle, nor did he try out for football or basketball, both teams on which Nick excelled. It was probably just as well since Max Watson was on the football team, too, and did his best to exploit the weak points of the other members.

While they had never been best friends, Nick and Jerry had come to like and respect each other. So Nick was pleased when they were sent to Sicily together.

And their trips into the countryside had cemented a friendship that would last forever. It was for this reason he had searched for a way to do something special for this quiet, unassuming buddy.

While Nick felt at home among the people and customs here he knew there were times when Jerry missed talking with others who shared his belief system. Their different beliefs and traditions were never discussed. There were too many points on which they were in complete agreement. But sometimes Nick glanced a flicker of yearning in Jerry's face as they visited small chapels out in the countryside and great cathedrals in the cities.

When Nick stopped the jeep in front of a small dwelling that looked as though it had been there for centuries, Jerry turned to him in surprise. "What's up? Why are we stopping here?"

"I've got a surprise for you." Nick's grin grew wider as he reached behind the seat and lifted out a cardboard box. "Come on," he laughed as he knocked on an ancient wooden door.

The woman who opened the door was dressed in a well-worn, well-scrubbed gray dress with a navy blue shawl around her shoulders. Her white hair was pulled back into a bun at the base of her neck and her face was creased with wrinkles. But her deep brown eyes were alive with life and merriment and curiosity.

"Buon giorno," she said quietly, the inflection at the end a question as well as a greeting.

"Buon giorno, signora," Nick replied. Then, in lilting Italian too rapid for Jerry to follow, explained their visit gazing from Jerry's puzzled expression to her's as he spoke.

A smile lit up her face as she stepped back and invited them into her humble home. It was a single room with a cot that Jerry knew must double as a bed in one corner. A small paint-chipped table with two wooden stools stood in the center of the room. An old wood stove was at the back wall with a small sink under a window next to it. A single light hung on a bare electric cord from the ceiling. She reached to it and turned on the switch. The low watt globe added to the light from the window casting a soft glow over the room.

Jerry's eyes were drawn to a book in the center of the table. Gold leaf letters, LIBRO DI MORMON, reflected the light against the black leather of the cover. He slowly faced the woman standing quietly there, "Lei é Mormone?"

"Si, é vero."

Then she began to speak rapidly in Italian as Nick, just as rapidly, interpreted for Jerry. She was born in a village near Torino. As a young woman she moved into Torino to be a governess for a family there. While there she met a handsome young student and he invited her to join him in lessons he was taking from two missionaries from America. They were both converted.

They were married and lived in Torino until Ettore, her husband, was drafted into the Italian army to fight with the Allies against the Central Powers which included Germany, Austria-Hungary, Bulgaria and the Ottoman Empire. Caterina's family had disowned her for her religious decision so she and her infant daughter were invited to live once again with the family in Torino and continue to teach their younger children.

After the war, Ettore and Caterina moved to Gratteri and lived with his family until their move to Mistretta. By this time they also had a son. While they were in Gratteri they met and studied with a small group at the home of Vincenzo Di Francesca. This continued on a monthly basis after their move to Mistretta but these meetings were banned after Italy allied itself with Germany in 1940 and the German military stationed troops in Sicily.

What about her husband and children, Jerry asked. Nick turned to Signora Perino and asked the question quietly.

Her eyes glistened with tears as she explained that her daughter, Isabella, had moved to America in 1938 and was married and living in California. The last letter Caterina had received from her included a photograph of Isabella and her husband, Lloyd, and their two children.

She showed them a black and white snapshot of a smiling young family standing in front of a small bungalow as she explained that she didn't know if Lloyd was now in the armed services. No mail had been delivered from America for nearly four years now.

As for her husband and son, Guido, they had been conscripted by the German army and sent to the Russian front. She didn't know where they were or if either of them was still alive. "Questa guerra é pessima," she whispered.

The two airmen nodded in agreement. The war *was* terrible.

Then Nick lifted the box he had carried in from the jeep and showed Signora Perino the food inside. "Per lei," he said, smiling.

A rush of Italian, including surprise and gratitude, poured from her lips as tears rolled freely down her face. Whatever Jerry couldn't comprehend from her words he understood from her expression. His eyes held questions as he looked at Nick.

"I'll explain later," Nick said.

As they continued to converse, Caterina invited them to sit on the two stools on either side of the table while she moved back and forth between a small cupboard and the table, preparing lunch for them. When everything was ready she quietly said, "Mangiate." Eat.

Jerry and Nick hesitated. They knew she was sharing with them food she desperately needed for herself.

"Mangiate," she said again. "Per favore."

They understood her desire to share her small store with them. This was her way of thanking them for the food they had brought and for their visit.

While they ate she asked questions about them and their families at home. She smiled when Nick spoke of the two of them growing up in a small town in Utah together. She nodded with a faraway look in her eyes, remembering her own children and their friends growing up here in Mistretta.

"É lei Mormone, anche?" she asked Nick.

He grinned, "No. Io sono Cattolico."

She looked from one to the other of them, seeing their friendship and recognizing that it had grown beyond religious differences. This pleased her. She murmured that perhaps there was hope for mankind, after all. When Nick translated this for Jerry, they both smiled in agreement.

~ ~ ~

As Nick carefully steered around the many curves on their way out of Mistretta, Jerry said, "That was great. How did you know about her?"

"You know Paolo?"

"You mean that kid who helps out in the mess?"

"Yes. One day when I was talking to him he asked me where in America I came from. When I said Utah, he perked up and told me about Signora Perino. He was born in Mistretta. I thought you'd like to meet her so I had Paolo give me directions to her house. Cookie heard and offered the food."

"Thanks, Nick. Visiting her was almost like being home again." Nothing more was said as they headed back out into the countryside on their way back to the base.

As they rounded a bend in the narrow road, the windshield of the jeep exploded as a bullet tore through it. Taken by surprise, Nick jerked the steering wheel trying to control the vehicle as it careened into a shallow depression and came to a halt. Both men jumped out and dropped to the ground as their eyes searched the hillside for the shooter.

Behind them, at the top of the low hill, rose a lone figure dressed in a ragged German uniform. He raised his gun and fired again. Jerry felt a searing pain in his side as Nick aimed his gun and, covering Jerry's body with his own, fired rapidly. Before the figure at the top of the hill dropped from sight, Nick's body jerked then grew limp.

The silence was both welcome and ominous. "Nick! Nick! Are you okay?" Jerry groaned as he slid from underneath his friend. Nick lay still, his shirt covered in blood.

"Nick! Hang on buddy! Hang on! Don't quit now!"

A low moan issued from Nick's lips as blood ran from the corner of his mouth.

Desperate to get help for Nick, Jerry tried to ignore his own pain as he lifted and maneuvered his friend into the jeep. He glanced over his shoulder as he struggled, keeping a watchful eye out for the sniper, but there was no further sign of movement on the hill.

Once Nick was in the vehicle, Jerry rocked the jeep until he was able to free it from the depression. Then he drove at breakneck speed down the narrow road to the base.

As Jerry was recuperating, he was given word that a group of American soldiers found the place where the German was hiding. He had been hit by one of Nick's bullets but was not mortally wounded. He was very young, still in his teens when he was captured. Once he realized the Americans were not going to kill him, he explained to the interpreter that he had been left behind when his comrades pulled out and had been hiding in an old, abandoned stone barn since, scrounging for food wherever he could find it. He had been foraging when he saw the jeep and assumed they were looking for him. Having been trained never to surrender, he made the decision he would not be taken without a fight.

When Jerry was deemed fit to return to duty he was transferred with his unit to a base near Rome which was now under Allied control. Before he left Sicily, he visited the small cemetery near the base. As he stood at the head of Nick's grave, he vowed that once this war was over and he was back home again, he would never raise his hand in anger. He also promised Nick he would tell his parents how their son, Nicholas Grosso, had died a hero.

When the war in both Europe and the Pacific came to an end Jerry was able to return home. Taking advantage of the G.I. Bill he enrolled at B.Y.U. in Provo and resumed his relationship with Emma which had been put on hold.

On one of his trips to Grassville while he was still in school his aunt handed him a letter. "This came for you a few days ago. We knew you were coming so didn't send it on." Jerry didn't recognize the town on the postmark or the handwriting on the envelope.

"Dear Mr. Harris," the letter began, "you don't know me but I want to thank you for what you did for my mother in Mistretta."

The letter went on to tell how, when mail service was finally restored between the U.S. and Italy, Caterina Perino and her daughter were able to correspond once again. In one of her letters Caterina wrote about the two young American airmen who had brought her food and hope. She had carefully written their names and hometown so when the war ended she would be able to tell Isabella about them. She didn't speak English but hoped her daughter would write and convey her gratitude.

"Non dimenticherò mai," she wrote. I'll never forget them.

When Jerry got back to Provo he read the letter to Emma and explained the trip he and Nick had taken to Mistretta. She knew Nick had been killed in the war but until that moment had not known the whole story.

From this letter grew a continuing correspondence between Isabella and Lloyd, and Jerry and Emma. They discussed their families, occupations and dreams.

One summer Jerry and Emma took their children to California to meet the Carsons. The two families traveled to the coast and rented rooms in a rustic seaside motel. While the children played at the water's edge, their parents reminisced and shared their latest news.

They talked about how Guido had come home at last and married his childhood sweetheart. The couple lived just a few doors away from Caterina and did as much as possible for this fiercely independent woman. He and his father had been separated as soon as they reached the Russian front and had never seen each other again.

Lloyd told of some of his experiences in the service in the Pacific. He had been stationed on Okinawa and Leyte before being sent to Tokyo with troops assigned there after the Japanese surrender agreement was signed.

Like Jerry, he didn't go into much detail about those years but one quiet afternoon on the beach as he and Jerry walked along the water's edge he told him that before he returned home he traveled with a group to Hiroshima.

"It still haunts my dreams," he said quietly.

After the Harris family returned home they heard from Isabella that Caterina, after miles of red tape and repeated inquiries, finally learned that Ettore had died that first terrible winter in Russia.

In later letters they learned that the Carson family traveled to Sicily twice before Caterina's death, so she did get to know her American grandchildren. And they never tired of hearing about the two young Americans who had been so good to her.

She had learned of Nick's death through village gossip and after Guido came home he drove her to the little cemetery to visit his grave. She wept as she placed flowers on his grave and later had Guido help her write a letter to Nick's parents to tell them how he had honored their name.

~ ~ ~

Emma's fingers joined Jerry's on the memorial plaque as they tenderly traced the letters spelling the name Nicholas Grosso one last time. Then, blinking back their tears they slowly walked back to join the others.

Chapter Three

"Emma?"

She turned at the sound of her name. "Yes?"

The room lights were dimmer than those in the hall from which she had just come and her macular degeneration made it difficult for her eyes to adjust rapidly. Jerry was talking to Walt a few feet away so couldn't be counted on to help identify the form standing before her.

"Yes?" she repeated.

"You don't recognize me do you?"

In that instant Emma's thoughts raced back to the scene around the kitchen table in her parents home years ago.

~ ~ ~

"Are you going to see her while you're here?"

"Yes, I'm planning to run over tomorrow while Jerry visits the Grossos. Does Robbie still have a drinking problem?"

"He doesn't see it as a problem, unfortunately, but yes, he does," Tom answered. "He lost his job at the mill because of it so Chuck put him on at the store as assistant manager but that didn't last. Then he tried having Robbie manage the drugstore but he botched that, too."

"When both their children started attending school all day, she took over managing the drugstore and Robbie helps out there whenever he's sober," Olivia added, "which isn't often. I feel so sorry for her. She looks old beyond her years but still stays with him."

"All she ever wanted was to be married to him," Emma said quietly. "He was a nice kid. Do you think going into the service caused him to start drinking?"

Jerry shook his head, "No. He started drinking while we were still in high school."

"I didn't know that." Emma looked intently at him, "How did you know?"

He grinned crookedly, "Well, you must have been the only one who didn't know. She knew, too, but she thought she could change him. I'm sorry for her that she couldn't."

~ ~ ~

"Ivy? Is it you?" By now Emma's eyes had adjusted to the soft lights and she could see the bitter grimace on her friend's once-lovely face.

"Of course it's me!" The sarcasm Emma remembered so well was still there. But the beauty and vibrancy were gone. "You don't have to look so shocked. You're no spring chicken yourself, you know."

Emma shook her head sadly. Been there, done that, she thought. And I won't bicker with her again. We're both too old and tired for that. "I'm sorry I didn't recognize you at first Ivy. You're right about the spring chicken bit, my eyes aren't what they used to be."

Ivy's faced softened slightly, "I'm sorry, too, Em. I'm so used to defending myself I got carried away. No hard feelings?"

"Right. No hard feelings. It's been a long time. How are you?"

"Just peachy keen, as you can see." As Ivy continued it was clear she had had cosmetic surgery once too often. The skin on her face was pulled so tight it appeared porcelain. Her once beautiful auburn hair was now a brassy scarlet and teased and lacquered in a high bouffant. Her tight magenta dress, which would clearly have been more appropriate on a high school student, clashed with her hair and made her skin look muddy.

"Remember those wonderful days when we were growing up?" She paused for emphasis, "Well they just keep getting better!"

Selective memory is still alive and well, Emma thought. I wonder if Ivy has a clue about the real world.

Ivy continued, the bright note in her voice ringing false, "Lily's daughter is the head cheerleader at her school and Charley's son is a football star just like his dad...and Robbie." She paused, trying to decide how much to say. Emma must have heard stories about Robbie by now so she just as well confront it, "Robbie has quit drinking. Things just couldn't be better."

"I'm glad," Emma said, meaning it more than Ivy would ever realize. If Ivy survives by living a fantasy life, far be it from me to disabuse her. "Are you still working?"

"Of course. When dad left the store and drugstore to Daisy and me she didn't want anything to do with it, so I bought her out." Her laugh was hollow, "We don't really need the money but managing them keeps me young."

Emma swallowed a smile. "Is Robbie here? I haven't seen him."

"Yes. He's probably tied up with some of his old buddies. Although I can't imagine why he keeps in touch with some of them. They're old."

~ ~ ~

"Come on Rob, pass it around."

"Get your own Max. You still owe me for the last time."

"Hey, old buddy, you know I'm good for it. I'll have your money by Tuesday for sure."

Robbie passed the white powder over to Max. "Okay, but this is the last time. If I don't get my money up front from now on there'll be no deals."

"Don't be such jerk. Didn't I save your life in Paris that time?"

"I wouldn't have been there at all if you hadn't got me drunk as a skunk. And you knew it when you took me there. You told me her old man was still a Kraut prisoner."

"I thought he was. How could I know his camp had been liberated." He leered wickedly, "We had a helluva time in old Paree, didn't we."

Both men grinned as they walked back inside.

"Watch it, jerk!"

"Sorry, I didn't see you."

"Is that you, Jer?" Robbie sniffed and wiped his runny nose with the back of his hand. "Damn, old buddy, it's good to see you. When did you get here?"

"About an hour ago."

"You missed all the fun this afternoon. We had a great time out on the links. Don't you still golf?"

"Yes." Jerry could see how raw it was around Robbie's nose and his eyes were bloodshot. "But we couldn't make it earlier."

Robbie grinned, "You mean the little lady wouldn't cut you loose for some good times with your old classmates?"

"It wasn't that . . ." but Robbie cut him off, "Em always was a good watchdog. If my old lady tried that I'd cut her loose in a minute."

Jerry turned away determined not to get sucked into an ugly discussion with an obviously impaired addict.

He worked his way over to where Emma stood talking to someone he didn't recognize at first glance. As he got closer he realized who it was. In spite of all her nips and tucks and color jobs, she looked old and brittle.

"Hi, Ivy. I just ran into Robbie."

"Well, aren't you the luckiest person alive. Oops, sorry Jerry, didn't mean to be rude. Em and I have been having a nice visit. It's too bad we don't see you oftener."

"Well, you know how it is. Life just gets busier." He turned to Emma, "How about it honey, ready to dance some more?"

"Love to." Emma hoped she didn't sound too anxious to get away from Ivy and her prattling. "See you later, Ivy."

As Jerry took her in his arms Emma was astonished at the envy in Ivy's eyes. Then it was replaced by a shrug and look of scorn, "Right, see you later."

"What got into her?"

"What do you mean?"

"When you told her you ran into Robbie she got awfully defensive."

Jerry sighed, "It would appear there's more trouble in paradise than we'd heard."

"I know she laid it on thick about her kids but I thought Robbie really had quit drinking."

"Maybe he has but I'm afraid he's found something worse."

"What could be worse than a drunken husband?"

"One who's into hard drugs."

"Oh, my gosh. Do you think she knows?"

"From the way she acted I'd guess she's got a pretty good idea."

"Poor Ivy," Emma murmured, "she was the most beautiful girl in Grassville. And she had everything she ever wanted, including Robbie. I used to be so jealous when she got to stay out as late as she wanted and when she showed up with a new dress or new shoes every time she turned around. I had to put cardboard in my shoes to keep from scratching my feet on the dirt and nearly all my clothes were hand-medowns from my cousins. I thought she had it all. Now I wouldn't trade places with her for all the money in the world."

"She might have had more things than you did but you're wrong about her being the most beautiful girl in town. You were."

Emma laughed, "Not prejudiced are you?"

"Not a bit. You had her beat hands down every way you turned."

"Well, I sure didn't know it then." She hesitated, "I wonder how much truth there is in what she said about her kids."

~ ~ ~

Charley Banks marched into the police station with fire in his eyes. "What the hell's going on here? Where's my kid?"

"He's in the other room. Before we bring him out we need to ask you some questions. Sit down, please."

The detective took the seat opposite and proceeded to ask Charley how much he knew about Chucky's actions over the past few months.

"He's out with friends most nights after football practice," Charley said proudly. "He's the best player on the team... just like his old man. You already know that."

"Are you aware he won't be playing when school starts?"

"What are you talking about? He's the best quarterback they've got. What do you mean he won't be playing?"

Detective Thomas shook his head, "He got kicked off the team nearly a month ago."

"The hell you say! Let me see my son!"

"Soon. Tell me where he got the money in a toolbox in the trunk of his car."

"Money? Toolbox? There's no law against keeping cash in your own car. Maybe he keeps a few bucks out of sight so his buddies won't take advantage of him."

The detective waited. "Does he have a job?"

"My kid's not gonna work till he needs a real job. After he gets outta school. I give him a few bucks spending money and his grandma supplies him if he needs more. You know a popular kid like him needs things to impress his friends. And the girls. There's not a damn thing wrong with him carrying a few bucks around in a toolbox."

"We're not talking about a few bucks, Mr. Banks. We're talking about nearly five thousand dollars."

"Five thou . . . I don't believe you. You're trying to trump up something against him. No way would he have that kinda money!"

"That's what we thought, too."

"And what did you get in his trunk for? Did you have a search warrant?"

"We didn't need one. He ran a red light and crashed into a semi truck. One of our men was at the intersection and saw it all. Chucky jumped out of his car, grabbed the toolbox out of the trunk and took off. He didn't get far before we tackled him. When he went down, the toolbox lid popped open and the money fell out. All new hundred dollar bills, banded and sorted just like they came straight from a bank."

Charley sat with his mouth open. No way! There has to be some mistake! "I don't know where the money came from. Maybe somebody planted it in his car. Where does he say it came from?"

"That's the problem. He won't talk. Maybe he'll tell you."

Detective Thomas stood and walked to the door. "You can bring him in now."

~ ~ ~

"Rob, come with me."

"What do you want now? I'm not giving you any more. I told you that."

Max's big hand grasped Robbie's arm as he pulled him out of the auditorium. "I don't want anything. Just come with me. I got something to tell you. Now!"

Half dragging him, Max shoved Robbie into an alcove under the stairs.

"What the hell do you think you're doing? Let go of me!"

Max turned his friend to face him. "I just heard. They've got Chucky down at the police station."

"You're full of crap." Robbie turned to force his way past Max.

"I'm telling you what I know. They've picked up your precious little Chucky."

Robbie's mind was blurry. He had a hard time comprehending what Max was saying. He saw his mouth moving but couldn't make out the meaning of the words. Something about Chucky and the police.

But that couldn't be true. Sheriff Dexter was his buddy. They'd been in the war together. He wouldn't drag his grandson to the station. Robbie had supplied money for Dex's campaign two years ago. Okay, so it was Ivy's money.

So what. It was the same thing. He shook his head trying to clear it.

At last the words started to make sense. The more he heard the more he realized they were in deep shit. Chucky had been picked up with a pile of cash.

"I gotta get out of here and find Ivy."

"What are you talking about? What does she have to do with this?"

Robbie stared at Max in amazement. "What does she have to do with this," he mocked, "What does she have to do with this? You're dumber than you look. Get out of my way!"

With that he shoved past his companion and hurried back to the auditorium.

Jerry and Emma danced past him but he didn't see them. His eyes searched wildly for Ivy but she was nowhere to be seen.

~ ~ ~

"Jerry did you see Robbie rush past? He looks frantic."

"Yes, I did see him." A memory of their early days together flashed into his mind. He had seen Robbie like that when he saw his dad talking to him after his mother was taken to the hospital. "He looks like he needs a friend. What about it, are you game?"

"Sure. What've we got to lose except a life-long friendship." They hurried after Robbie.

But before they could reach him they saw two policemen walk in the door. They looked around the room then separated and walked around the perimeter of the room never taking their eyes off the dancing couples.

The first policeman reached Robbie and said something quietly to him. Robbie's shoulders drooped as he shuffled in front of the officer toward the door.

Then they watched as the second policeman approached Ivy dancing with Walt. He leaned in close and whispered something to her. She shook her head slowly and her grip on Walt tightened. Even from where they were they could see her face turn to stone.

Walt stopped dancing, looking questioningly from Ivy to the policeman. The officer said something else. It was obvious it was meant for Walt as well as Ivy.

She held onto Walt until it was embarrassing to watch. Walt's face darkened as he tried to break her grip but she continued to cling to him saying, "Go away! Can't you see we're dancing?"

Jerry and Emma reached the trio. Emma gently touched Ivy's arm and whispered, "Ivy, what's wrong?"

"Nothing's wrong, girly-girl. Don't touch me. We're trying to dance in peace here."

Walt continued to struggle to break loose from her grip. His face was crimson. He muttered, "Get her off me and out of here."

Jerry and the police officer stepped forward to shield the couple from the gaze of curious dancers nearby while Emma repeated Ivy's name again. "Come on. Let's go get a breath of fresh air."

Ivy suddenly took her arms from around Walt's neck and turned on Emma, "Don't you dare tell me what to do! Or where to go! You always were jealous of me cause I was popular and you weren't! Just get out of my way, little miss goody two shoes! I don't need you!"

Emma stepped back, stunned, not knowing what to do.

Jerry put his arm around Emma as the officer took Ivy firmly by the arm. He was suddenly joined by the first policeman. The two of them took Ivy between them and inched her toward the door repeating, "Come on, Mrs. Banks. We need you to come with us." Their voices were gentle but rimmed with steel. They knew the drill. They had done this before.

"Jerry, come on," Emma said, "we've got to try and help her."

"It won't do any good, Emma," Walt's voice shook. "It looks like her grandson and husband have finally been caught."

"What do you mean?"

"Everybody in town knows they've been dealing in drugs. We've all wondered how long Dex was going to turn away from doing his job." Walt paused, "From what Shorty just said, it's finally hit the fan."

"Did Ivy know?"

Walt laughed sourly, "Ivy knows what Ivy wants to know. In her heart she'll always be the homecoming queen. She never got beyond her high school years. She'd be pitiful if she wasn't so self-centered."

Jerry put his hand on Walt's shoulder. "I'm sorry it took so long to pry her off you. Are you okay now?"

"Yeah, I'm fine. Thanks for helping. Gotta go get some of that fresh air you were talking about. See you later."

"Feel like dancing some more?" Jerry's voice was gentle.

"Maybe later. Let's go get something to drink. I think I need to sit down." Jerry and Emma made their way toward the punch bowl on a table near the back of the room.

Chapter Four

The strain was beginning to show in Emma's face. Jerry handed her a cup of juice and asked, "Are you okay? We can leave now if you want."

A warm smile brightened her eyes and seemed to lift her physically. The light glinting off her hair highlighted the few silver strands showing through. She had always thought of her hair as drab but the soft blond color of her youth had darkened to light brown over the years complementing her fair complexion. Her face was creased with the comfortable lines of increasing years, laugh lines dominant as a grin or chuckle was never far away.

Everything was a trade-off any more she was finding. Youthful vigor and brashness were replaced by a slower pace and caution. The old 'look before you leap' warnings made sense now. But she wouldn't go back. She smiled as she was reminded of a remark made by a friend as the group joked about the so-called golden years. "Oh, they're golden all right. It's just that the doctors get all the gold."

She looked into Jerry's soft, gentle brown eyes filled with such love and concern she was comforted and refreshed. Like hers, his hair was touched with-silver. His broad, strong face was filled with tenderness and humor, traits that had attracted her once she overcame her youthful insecurities and increased over their years together.

His parents had severely abused him before he was removed from their home and sent to live with his aunt and uncle. The physical scars had softened some over the years but were still visible. But Jerry was determined from the time he moved to Grassville and met Rebecca O'Brien, his seventh grade English teacher, and the Williams family, who had accepted him unconditionally, to erase the emotional scars which had been inflicted upon him. And he succeeded.

"Let's wait awhile longer." Mary had written that they were going to try and make it this year if possible. "Don't worry, hon, I'm fine. I just need to sit here and rest a bit. That business with Ivy and Robbie simply took me by surprise. I'll be okay in a minute."

"Well looky here! If it isn't Tweedle Dum and Tweedle Dee! I thought you two were too good to join us poor hicks."

The brash voice was instantly recognizable as Max sat down heavily across the table from Jerry and Emma, wiping his runny nose on the back of his hand and staring at them with red-rimmed eyes. The years had not been kind to him.

The more things change, the more they stay the same, thought Jerry. And it looks like he drinks from the same well Robbie does.

But he was determined not to get pulled into a tug of war with his old nemesis. "Ready to go, Emma?" he asked as he took her hand.

But Emma wasn't about to back down. Max had been the school bully all those years ago and the stories told about him in the years since hadn't improved his reputation. She decided it was time someone took him down a notch.

"Well, good old Max. Haven't lost your charm, have you?"

He was taken aback. In spite of his bluster he had always stood in awe of her. She was one of the few kids who wasn't afraid to stand up to him. He had asked her for dates more than once during their high school years but she would never agree to go out with him. And she hadn't bothered with excuses or evasions, either. "Drop dead!" had been her mildest response making her even more tempting to conquer. Because every girl was a conquest to him.

Once when a new kid moved to town he asked Max what the chance was of getting a date with Emma. "You can't touch her with a ten foot pole," had been his response.

Even after his shotgun marriage to Connie, Max had not given up hope of scoring with Emma. But she would have none of it.

"Ah, don't be a sorehead. I'm just surprised to see you." He fidgeted, "You didn't show up at the other reunions."

"And I'm sure you missed us," she said dryly.

"Sure," he stammered, "sure we missed you."

"We? Got a mouse in your pocket?"

He frowned. He never had been good at riddles. "Mouse? What In hell are you talkin' about? You makin' fun of me?"

"Moi?" Emma grinned, "Would I make fun of someone as upstanding and intelligent as you?"

Now he was truly confused. He thought he'd just been insulted but couldn't figure out how.

"Is Connie here tonight?" This time there was no mockery in Emma's voice.

"Naw. She never likes to have fun." He wasn't about to admit Connie had finally left him. And he didn't know where she was. But when he found her he planned to beat the living daylights out of her. His money never lasted the month any more and he was in hock up to his neck to Robbie.

~ ~ ~

Connie waited until the children left for school before she told Angie she would be leaving on the noon bus.

"Why, mom? You know you're welcome to stay here with us."

"I know that, Angie, but my job won't be there if I stay any longer."

"You don't need to keep working. We'll take care of you."

"Thanks, honey, I appreciate that. But I do need to keep working. I'll be eligible for higher social security benefits if I stay another year."

"Have you thought about going back with dad and getting in on his benefits?"

Connie tried to keep a straight face. If she went back to Max he'd use every cent of her money for drugs and women. Just like he'd been doing all their years together.

But she would not criticize him to his daughter. Angie didn't understand what life with Max had been like. The shame and humiliation. And utter hopelessness.

* * *

"No, Max. I don't want to."

"Come on Connie. You know you want it as much as I do."

And she did want it. But she was determined not to end up like her mother, gossiped about by the women in that self-righteous Ladies Hospitality club and bringing home any man that would give her a little money.

"I said no! Stop it!"

Max loved it when they struggled. It was even more fun than when they agreed. And plenty of them had agreed after he made the football team. In fact, the contest going on now was down to two. If Max scored tonight he'd be one ahead of George in the pool and wouldn't have to buy beer for a week.

~ ~ ~

"Pregnant! What the hell are you talking about?"

"You know what I'm talking about."

Yeah, he knew. But he wasn't about to take this lying down. His dad was the sheriff. He would fix it. "I'll say it's not mine. Nobody'll believe a Denton anyway."

But he was wrong. His dad did believe Helen Denton about Max and her daughter. "I don't understand you, boy. I purely don't. You could have anything you want."

"Well, I don't want to marry her."

"It's too late for that. You should have thought of that before you went down that sorry road."

Mrs. Watson stood in the background wringing her hands.

She could hear the club women laughing at her now. Dick was right. They had to get married right away.

~ ~ ~

Connie's sixteenth birthday was the best ever. That was the first time she had gone riding with Max. He was a senior and a star Sommerset High football player. She intended to try out for the cheerleading squad when she got to high school next year. Max said she'd be a cinch to make it.

She knew she stood a good chance. Her raven hair fell in soft waves around a pixie face. Long lashes surrounded beautiful emerald green eyes above a pert nose and full lips always in a smile. Like her mother, she had matured early filling out all the places that needed filling out. Her tiny waist could be spanned by Max's large hands and everyone said her legs were better than Betty Grable's.

But her hopes for cheerleading dissolved when her pregnancy could no longer be hidden and she was asked to leave school so she wouldn't be a bad example to the other girls. When she questioned why Max was allowed to finish and even graduate, her principal said, "It's not the same thing at all. Max has been a great asset to Sommerset High sports and he'll be a great asset to our country when he goes into the army and goes off to fight for our great country."

~ ~ ~

The young couple had been living with Max's parents but when he and his buddies left for war, Connie moved back with her mother. She saved every cent of the allotment checks that came every month so when Max came home they'd be able to buy a house of their own. She added to the money by working two jobs, one stocking shelves in the grocery store and the second one cleaning the theater after the last movie until the twins were born. The money from these jobs helped pay her share of expenses at home.

When Sean and Angie were two months old Connie's mother agreed to tend them from ten p.m. to the early morning hours so Connie could do janitor work at the confectionary and store plus her cleaning job at the theater. Her wages were minimal but without a high school diploma this was the best work she could hope to find, a fact that Mr. Greeley and theater manager, Colin Jones, reminded her of whenever she asked for a raise.

Sean looked exactly like Max with his broad smiling face, clear cobalt blue eyes and halo of golden curls. He was quiet and undemanding to care for. Angie, on the other hand looked more like her mother with her green eyes and black wavy hair and pixie face. But she was a difficult, colicky baby never sleeping more than two or three hours at a time, day or night. That they were both quick and clever was obvious by the time they were six months old but their personalities were as different as day and night.

Connie took the children to the Watsons every Sunday afternoon. Max's parents loved both of them but were unable to keep their favoritism for Sean hidden. They bought the children small treats from time to time and new outfits on their birthdays. But Mrs. Watson never offered to tend them or give Connie and her mother a break by taking them overnight. And her gifts to Sean were always more expensive than the things she gave Angie.

Connie tried to overlook this and as the children grew she made as much fuss over Angie's gifts from grandma Watson as she did Sean's. But Angie was a very bright child and recognized this trait in her grandma early. She also recognized her mother's attempts to hide her disappointment and never complained.

Sean eventually recognized it, too, and tried to make things right by sharing with his sister whatever grandma Watson gave him. Neither child talked of this with their mother or grandma Denton.

Max's enlistment was up the year the twins turned five.

~ ~ ~

"No, I don't want to buy a house in this two-bit town. I'm going to live in Sommerset."

"But Max, our families are here, we both grew up here, the children's friends are here."

"Tough. I'm heading for Sommerset. You can either tag along with me or stay here. I don't much care which you do."

Connie no longer recognized this Max. The one she knew before the war was no ball of kindness but the one standing before her now was a stranger. He ignored her and their children and seldom visited his parents, though his mother pled with him to at least come for dinner on Sunday.

Sommerset, like the rest of the country was enjoying a postwar boom in affordable housing. Their move in 1951 was to a small, two bedroom house in a new development just inside the city limits.

The money Connie had saved, plus a low-cost loan under the GI Bill made it possible for them to move in before Christmas. Connie looked forward to staying home with the children but that dream faded as Max moved from job to job, always complaining about someone at work who had it in for him or some aspect of the job that was beneath his worth.

By the following March Connie was once again holding down two all-night menial jobs. She put the twins to bed at 8 p.m. every night and left for the janitorial work she had found in a downtown office building and feedlot store. Max always promised to stay home all night but, too often, she came home to sleeping children with Max nowhere in sight.

The more she threatened to quit her jobs and live on whatever Max made the more he disappeared. Finally, in desperation she asked her mother to come and stay with them until September when the children would be in school all day and she could look for daytime work.

Helen promised the man she was currently living with that she would be home on weekends if he would stay. He encouraged her to go, glad for the chance to live in her house without having to make a commitment to marriage or be accountable to her during the week.

Max made no complaints. This freed him up to spend more time at the local bars and with the women available there.

By September Connie secured work as a maid in a motel not far from home and the new McDonald's constructed next door. She was able to get the children off to school, report at the motel and be finished there by 11:30 a.m. From there she rushed to the fast food cafe and cooked hamburgers and fries until the evening cook arrived.

Sean and Angie were instructed to come straight home from school and clean their room before settling down in front of the TV to await Connie's arrival home to cook supper and work with them on their homework.

Max's job pattern remained checkered sometimes working in town and other times claiming to have work in other areas. He would disappear for weeks on end only to appear at suppertime and act as if this was a normal way to live.

By the time the twins enrolled in high school, Max's part in their lives was negligible. Both children were on the honor roll every term, a fact which delighted Connie.

~ ~ ~

"Do you ever think about dad?"

"Not much. What do you mean?"

Angie sighed. "He's never been to any of our school programs or assemblies. Sally's and Maribeth's dads are around all the time. Sometimes they ask about dad."

"What do you tell them?"

"I change the subject."

"Well, I gave up on him years ago," Sean continued, "when he wanted me to get involved in sports and ignored me when he realized I wasn't interested."

Connie had been working at the Starlight Cafe three years when the twins started their junior year. The work was long, 6 a.m. to 6 p.m., six days a week but the tips were good. And most nights the cook slipped something into a bag for her to take home for their supper.

Connie's figure and legs were still good. Her raven hair was still lustrous and her emerald eyes still glowed with merriment and hidden promises. But her face was now developing lines and creases and she sometimes squinted when trying to distinguish words at a distance. It would be time for glasses soon, she knew, but didn't know how she would afford to pay for them.

She had taught Sean and Angie to cook, clean house and do the washing and ironing. But she didn't help them with their lessons anymore. Sometimes as she read essays they wrote or watched them complete pages of geometry, she ached to be learning what they were learning.

They saw it, too.

"Mom, why don't you go to night school and get your high school degree?"

"Aw, Sean, I'm too old for that."

"No, you're not," Angie said quietly. "You're not old at all. And you could do it. We'd help."

So Connie began night classes sixteen years after she had been asked to leave school in Grassville. The twins were true to their word and helped her in every way possible.

But she didn't need help with assignments and papers and tests. She reveled in the knowledge she was acquiring and the feeling of self worth that accompanied it.

Max made fun of her efforts when he learned what she was doing but she was determined not to be stopped. She received her high school diploma the week before Sean and Angie graduated.

They both received scholarships to the University of Utah. "Come to Salt Lake with us," they coaxed.

But Connie knew it was time for them to flex their wings without her constant supervision. And she was offered a job in a real estate office in Sommerset that she was anxious to try. A job in the same building she had once cleaned as a janitor.

"Maybe someday I'll move there," she said, "but not yet." She had not given up entirely on Max. Maybe, with her encouragement, he would once again be the man with whom she had fallen in love.

Three years later she discovered Max and Robbie Banks were working a scam on elderly couples. They were promising to replace worn out roofs with new shingles at a fraction of the cost offered anywhere else.

But the finished product was not a new roof, merely the old roof painted with a special oil that made it look new.

~ ~ ~

"First you have to stop the scam then work to repay the money you took from those people."

"Or what?"

"Or I'll turn you in." The coldness in her voice and eyes told Max it was not an idle threat.

"Nobody'll believe you. My dad might be retired but he's still got plenty of friends in law enforcement."

"He's the first one I'll tell."

Max remembered the look on his dad's face when he told him he *would* marry Connie Denton. He backed down.

But he didn't replace the money he had taken from the people who had believed him. So, feeling sorry for the couples who had barely enough to live on as it was, Connie quietly and over a period of time paid them all back out of her own wages. Max never knew she had done this.

By the mid 1980s, Connie had once again built up a comfortable nest egg through savings and investments Max knew nothing about. She had watched through the years as he lied and cheated his way through one shady deal after another.

She knew about his women, his drinking and his drug deals with Robbie. He was seldom at home and when he did show up she knew to keep her purse hidden. He had pawned everything he could lay his hands on.

Since the house was in both their names he could not touch that until she was ready to make her move.

~ ~ ~

Angie and her husband and children were living in a beautiful home in Logan.

Sean had never married but had kept in close touch with his mother. "Don't you think it's time you seriously think about moving?"

"Yes, you're right. It is time." Connie laughed, "And I even have a job waiting for me in Salt Lake. That's close to you in Ogden and Angie in Logan. But not close enough for me to interfere in your lives."

"As if you would!"

Her laugh was relaxed and joyous, "Perhaps, but I don't want to be tempted."

"Does dad know?"

"No. And I'm not telling him. We've sold the house and he's taken off with his share of the money. When he returns to Sommerset I'll be long gone."

And so Sean and Angie both agreed not to tell their dad where their mother was now living. And they kept their word.

* * *

Max moved his head from side to side searching for someone he could hit up for his next fix if Ivy's lawyer couldn't spring Robbie. His glance fell on Luke. "Maybe he's still got some," he muttered.

Jerry and Emma glanced at Max, hearing him mumble but not understanding the words. They looked away in disgust.

"I'm ready to dance now," Emma said quietly to Jerry. She was beginning to feel soiled sitting near Max.

She knew where Connie was. She had run into her in a bookstore at Trolley Square a few months earlier. "You look great, Connie."

"Thanks." The strain was gone from her face and everything about her was more buoyant, more exuberant. "I feel great...never been better. It's so good to see you again."

They found a quiet place and talked at length about the old days growing up in Grassville. They talked about their children and grandchildren and shared favorite books and authors. "Are you still living in Sommerset?"

"No," Connie grinned. And then she told Emma.

Chapter Five

"There's Mary."

She stood at the entrance expectantly. Her hair was now snowy white framing a face as smooth as a young girl's. Her black eyes danced as she caught sight of her friends.

"You came! I was afraid you wouldn't be able to make it." They embraced then stepped apart, enjoying the closeness they had shared since becoming fast friends back in Rebecca's seventh grade English class.

Emma placed her hand on her friend's shoulder her eyes filled with compassion and concern. "Was the trip too much for Rick?"

Mary reached up to accept Jerry's hug before turning once again to Emma. "No. He's feeling much better now. That open heart surgery took a lot out of him but he's tough and was determined not to let it get the best of him. We took our time coming from Taos, and stopped early every day so he could get out and walk around before turning in.

"We saw such beautiful country. Every mile I thought of the poem you sent after your trip through southern Utah and Arizona."

Emma smiled, remembering the images that had spoken to her soul on that long journey through the desert. As a child one summer she had traveled with her family from Grassville to Blanding. She remembered the countryside as drab and barren, with sparse vegetation and searing heat.

Then, one beautiful spring five years ago, she and Jerry drove through that same countryside, across Monument Valley through the Navajo Indian Reservation to Flagstaff, on to Tucson and then to Yuma. Her eyes changed and her heart was opened to the stark beauty surrounding them and she wrote:

> The Desert: at first glance desolation,
> on closer look, inspiration.
> Arches, crags, sentinels and more
> rising from the desert floor
> standing watch, silent guard duty
> clothed in indescribable beauty
> reaching far and reaching wide
> shapes and forms on every side,
> monuments to God above
> who blessed this earth with so much love.
> And colors pure from rose to blue
> cloaked in shades of every hue.
> Brilliant sky, blazing sun,
> then clouds roll in, one by one
> and as they pass, vistas change
> from simple to stark to surreal, strange
> until every butte and every spire
> is aflame with moving, living fire.
> Saguaros standing proud and high
> with arms outreaching toward the sky.
> Tiny flowers on prickly pears,
> stunted trees waiting unawares
> for those long gone to return anew
> to terraces, dwellings they once knew.
> Of all the beauty in all the world,
> the desert shows God's love unfurled.

Emma grinned crookedly, "That's nice of you to say so. I debated about sending it then figured you were a good enough friend you wouldn't hold it against me."

"Hold it against you?" Mary smiled. "I love it."

Needing to change the subject Emma asked, "Have you had time to paint since Rick's surgery?"

"Not at first. I needed to be available. But once he started feeling better he encouraged me to go back to the studio." The same shy look Emma remembered from their youth when Mary showed her the beautiful handiwork she had made flashed across her face. "I've got a show coming up soon. All my work from the last show has been sold."

"That's great." Jerry added, "I'm not surprised. You're very good. Are your new paintings desert scenes, too?"

"Yes. That's where my heart is." She turned to Emma, "You remember me telling you my dad saying he never wanted to forget the beautiful colors of New Mexico?"

Emma nodded.

"Well, once I saw it, I knew what he meant. I'm so glad they got to move back after he retired. They lived in Tularosa but we got down to see them or they came up and stayed with us a couple of times a year before they died."

Mary glanced down the hall, "Rick should be coming along pretty soon. We stopped to see the Memorial and he wanted to stay there awhile longer. He recognized nearly all the names. I figured he needed time alone so came on looking for you."

~ ~ ~

Rick read through the names once again. So many, he thought, so many from such a small area. There were only a few names he didn't recognize. He stood at attention, taps playing silently in his head, as one face after another floated gently by. Then he quickly brushed his eyes with the back of his hand and turned toward the sound of music and voices.

* * *

"Who's that sweeping the porch?" He was looking at the house behind the mill office.

Abe glanced out the window. "That's Luis Ruiz's girl."

"Is he the one that made that nice rocking chair for ma?"

"That's him. Pretty little thing, isn't she."

Before Rick could answer, Molly stepped in saying, "Supper's ready. Come and get it."

They ate without talking, each one hesitant to broach the topic bothering them all.

As she passed the dessert around Molly said, "I made your favorite...pineapple pie."

"Thanks ma." And then he saw the tears. "Please ma. You said you wouldn't cry."

"I'm trying not to," her voice quivered, "but you going away to war is killing me."

Abe patted her hand. "Now mother, don't make this any harder than it is."

Molly shook her head, determined to do what generations of women had done before her. Keep a stiff upper lip.

~ ~ ~

Rick, with the U.S. Marines under Major General Vandergrift, landed on Guadalcanal in the Solomon Islands on August 7, 1942. The fighting was terrible and control of the island fluctuated between Allied and Japanese troops for several months. It wasn't until February 1943 when army troops under General Patch joined the battle that Guadalcanal was finally cleared.

"What did you say that is called?"

"Bushido," Rick answered.

Lloyd shook his head. This was the first time any of them had encountered the fanatical code which required Japanese soldiers to fight to the death.

Rick added, "The code goes back a long time. They've been taught since childhood that surrender means disgrace, to lose face, and those who truly believe choose suicide over capture."

During the Solomoms campaign the Allies perfected the technique of amphibious warfare, involving air, land and sea forces working as a team. This was the beginning of many jungle campaigns, also. Heavy rains rendered roads unusable causing troops to wade through knee-deep, thick, black mud. In the murky half-light soldiers often could not differentiate their own battle lines from the enemy's.

Many servicemen contracted Malaria and other jungle diseases which took a terrible toll. And added to this wretchedness was the danger of Japanese snipers lurking everywhere.

~ ~ ~

"Any word today, mother?"

Molly sighed, "Nothing."

Rick's last letter was dated weeks before and so many words were censored out, it was difficult to read.

"I almost hate to go downtown anymore."

Abe knew what she meant. More blue stars were appearing in windows daily, meaning more boys had gone off to war. But worse than the blue stars were those that had been replaced by gold stars indicating sons or brothers or husbands who had been killed in action.

Abe thought of his stint in the army during World War I, the war to end all wars it had been called. He had never talked much about the conditions in the trenches across

France and Belgium but he had never forgotten them, either. In his heart he hoped Rick's situation was different but his intellect told him this was wishful thinking. War is terrible in any form.

~ ~ ~

The fighting moved from one location to another. The tumult and clamor was unending. Rick wondered if he would ever erase the sights and sounds from his consciousness. *Was it this bad for dad,* he wondered? Realizing for the first time how silent Abe had been on his service in the military.

With his company Rick landed on Kwajalein the last day of January 1944 and after a week of fierce fighting occupied the atoll. It was nearly a month before Enewetak atoll came under Allied control.

A new bomber, the B-29, half again as large as the B-17 bombers blasting Germany, had been developed by the army air forces. The Mariana Islands were in long range distance of Japan so the Allied command knew it was essential to occupy these islands for use as bases for these superfortress bombers.

Thus, once again Rick was sent to battle. Under the command of Lt. General H. M. Smith, marine and army troops occupied Saipan in July. In this battle there were nearly 16,500 Allied casualties and 28,000 enemy soldiers dead.

But there was neither time for regret nor jubilation as army and marine forces invaded Guam and it was announced on August 10 that organized resistance there ended. The army promptly built huge bases in these islands and the first B-29 raid on Japan from these bases took place in November.

~ ~ ~

"Good morning. Mama wants you and Mr. Kenner to have this. It's a special Christmas cake that has been passed down in her family for generations."

"Tell your mother thanks. I'm sure we'll enjoy it. It's nice to see you, Mary." Molly smiled as she took the cake, "Are you home from school for the holidays?"

"Yes, the term ended last Friday." Mary glanced at the dry ground outside the house, "I like snow for Christmas but I'm so glad the roads were dry so dad could come to Salt Lake and get me."

"How do you like the U?"

"It's great. The art department is incredible."

"Rick went there for two years before he transferred to the college in Logan."

Mary hesitated, wondering how to approach what was on her mind. She had seen Rick a few times on his visits home before the war but had never met him. "How is he? Do you hear from him much?"

"Not as often as I'd like. His letters are dated at fairly regular intervals but they don't get here for a long time after they're written."

Go on, scaredy cat. Say what's on your mind. "Uh, um, some of us at school have formed a group to write to our servicemen. Do you think Rick would be interested in hearing from any of us?"

Molly smiled, her eyes bright with compassion. She knew how hard this was for Mary to ask. Mary was always pleasant and polite but her manner was quiet and reserved, bordering on shyness. "I think he'd be delighted."

The young woman was already regretting her boldness.

Mrs. Kenner was probably laughing at her foolishness seeing it as a bumbling attempt to get acquainted with her handsome son. Her blush deepened to scarlet, burning her cheeks.

But before she could undo the damage, Molly was writing Rick's APO address and handing it to Mary. "I think it's wonderful that you young people are patriotic enough to think of our boys. Rick writes that mail call is the high point in their lives. I'm sure he'll answer whoever writes. Just be sure to tell your friends to be patient. Mail service from our boys is slow at best and shut down for weeks at a time at worst. But, so far, we've received each others letters on a fairly regular basis."

~ ~ ~

"We're on our way again."

"Do you know our destination?" Lloyd asked.

"I know our army air forces and navy have been bombing and shelling Iwo Jima daily for months now to take out as many concrete fortifications and underground defense systems as possible to try to make our job easier."

February 19, 1945, Schmidt's Fifth Marine Amphibious Corps landed on Iwo Jima. They met savage opposition from Japanese troops stationed there. Four days later marines climbed the steep slopes of Mount Suribachi and hoisted the American flag.

As Rick and Lloyd watched the flag their hearts filled with pride. But they knew the battle was not over, that fierce fighting still lay ahead before Iwo Jima was secure.

They were right. It took twenty-six more days of bitter fighting before Iwo Jima came under Allied control.

"Mail call!" As the servicemen circled, he called out, "Marsh, R.J.; Carson, Lloyd; Kenner, Rick. . ." the names continued as Rick took his letters and walked over to a quiet spot away from the others.

> Dad keeps busy all the time, just like
> always. Do you remember Joe Hoffstein?
> Dad's put him in charge of all lathe
> jobs. Says he's one of his best workers.

We sold your motorcycle like you asked and added it to the money coming in from your allotment checks. There'll be a small nest egg to help till you get a job when you come home. I know you can't tell us where you are but we're certainly keeping our prayers going for you.
Love, Mom

There were two other letters, one from his cousin stationed in England and another one in handwriting he didn't recognize. He read the letter from his cousin first then turned his attention to the third letter.

~ ~ ~

"Hi, Mary, ready to go?"
"Yes." She took a small parcel from the table and walked out the door with Emma.
"I'll bet you made something for the baby, didn't you?"
"I knitted a sweater and booties," Mary smiled.
"It figures," Emma said ruefully. "I bought a couple of receiving blankets. I tried to knit something like you taught me years ago but it turned out tacky, as usual."

~ ~ ~

"Hey, you guys. I'm glad you could make it." Ivy grinned proudly, "Here he is, my little Charles Robert." She pulled the blanket away from the baby's face. "Doesn't he look just like his daddy?"
Emma and Mary tickled the baby's chin trying to get him to smile. "He does," Mary said.
"How is Robbie?" Emma asked. "Do you have any idea where he is?"
"Somewhere in Europe, but we don't know where for sure. He was stationed in England for awhile but once he left

there all mention of his whereabouts have been censored out of his letters. He's mentioned Max a couple of times so I assume they're in the same area. I asked Max's mother if they know where he is, but they don't know, either."

"What do you hear from Daisy? Does she like the WAVES?"

A sour look crossed Ivy's face so like the look her mother always had when talking about "that Denton woman" or Sally Oliver, "Who knows? She hardly ever writes."

Daisy had been a pariah in the Greeley family ever since she became pregnant in the ninth grade and had to move to Denver to keep people in Grassville from finding out. Of course it wasn't long before the truth about her became common knowledge but that didn't slow Agatha Greeley's tongue for long.

Even before the war started Daisy was rebellious, constantly trying to distance herself from her family. But Chuck Greeley's money made it possible for her to continue buying more trinkets and clothes than she could afford if she moved out so she continued to live at home.

Then she saw a poster about the Navy's female auxiliary called the WAVES (Women Accepted for Voluntary Emergency Service) and decided this was the very chance she had been waiting for. She hoped to not only be able to support herself but be in close proximity to as many young servicemen as possible, too.

~ ~ ~

"These are beautiful," Emma exclaimed as she looked through the folder of watercolors Mary had brought home to show her parents. "I can see why you got that scholarship."

"Thank heavens I did. I would never have been able to go to school otherwise." She smiled that wonderful shy smile

Emma loved, "I'm the first one on both sides of my family to go to college. I can't possibly let my family down."

Mary pulled out a scene from the bottom, "Do you recognize this?"

Emma studied the picture carefully. "Of course. Have you been back since that infamous day six years ago?"

"No. That's from memory."

"But every detail is clear. I recognize every gnarled tree and clump of brush and slab of shale. How did you remember it so well?"

"Everything about that day is imprinted on my mind." She smiled, "We were there quite awhile, you remember."

Emma sighed, "How could I forget."

They were remembering the Easter when the two girls climbed the mountain above the picnic grounds and Emma brashly took one step too far and slid on the shale. Without the quick-thinking help of Jerry and Mary, Emma would have gone over the cliff to her death on the rocks below.

"It's too bad they stopped those Easter picnics when the war started."

"Yeah." Emma shook her head, "The war has changed so many things. I wonder if anything will ever be the same."

Mary laughed, "Please! You sound like my dear old grandma talking about the good old days."

"You're right. I can't believe I said that." She looked at her watch, "I better head for home. It's been great to see you. Definitely plan to stay a weekend with me in Provo next month. I'll show you some great scenery to add to your Salt Lake and Grassville pictures."

~ ~ ~

The battle to occupy Okinawa finally ended the third week in June. It proved to be exceedingly bloody. The ship carrying Rick and Lloyd was damaged by a kamikaze plane but was able to limp into harbor and unload the troops aboard.

"The way their men are fighting to the death, I don't see how there can be anybody left to fight by the time we reach Japan itself."

"I agree," Lloyd answered as they watched another pilot dive his plane into a ship. "That's beyond patriotism. I understand they believe their emperor is a god."

"I've heard that, too," Rick said tiredly. "Come on, let's change our socks and head out."

Lloyd nodded. Both marines had never forgotten two important fundamentals they learned in basic training: "Think of your rifle as your friend. Never point it at anybody unless you intend to pull the trigger." "Always carry a pair of dry socks. Jungle rot is deadly."

~ ~ ~

Mary turned the letter over in her hands. It had been so long since she wrote she wasn't sure she could remember what she said. She had chided herself dozens of times for being so presumptuous as to think he would want to hear from her. Some of her friends now had ongoing correspondence with the servicemen they had written to but Mary had never heard a word.

School would be out for the summer in another month and here was a letter. The postmark gave no clue as to when it had been mailed. She shook her head as she reached for her nail file and slowly slit open the envelope.

12 April 1945

Dear Mary Ruiz,
Your letter finally got to me. We've been busy. I don't know how much news you get at home about this part of the world and I can't

write anything but I will tell you it was nice to hear from you. News from home is always welcome.

Yes, I do remember seeing you even though we haven't met. My dad thinks the world of your father and mom says your mother is a great cook.

Yes, I enjoyed my time at the U. It's a good school. I would've continued there but the forestry program I needed was in Logan. It's a good school, too.

Yes, I did get to work as a ranger before the war. I was told I can have my job back when it's over but I don't have any idea where I'll be sent. I worked in both Colorado and Idaho and liked both places. Since you're an art student I'll bet you'd love some of the scenery I saw.

Thanks again for writing. I would enjoy hearing from you again if you have time to write. Mom is right, mail call is the best part of being in the service.

Sincerely,
Rick Kenner

~ ~ ~

Abe hurried into the house. "Did you hear the news, mother?" He switched on the radio. "Germany surrendered!"

They listened as the disembodied voice said, "On the first of this month German radio announced Hitler died defending Berlin against the Russians but that has not been verified. Early yesterday morning, May 7, 1945, Jodl of the German high command signed the terms of unconditional surrender at Reims, France. Eisenhower's chief of staff,

Lt. General Walter B. Smith signed for the Allies. All across the free world V-E Day is being celebrated. After five years, eight months and seven days, the war in Europe is finally over!"

"Thank God," Molly murmured. "Now if we can just get Japan to surrender, our dear Rick can come home again."

~ ~ ~

"Did you hear about Hitler?"

"Yeah," Rick responded, "when they said he died in battle I wondered if we'd ever know the truth."

"Suicide," Lloyd said disgustedly, "it figures." He continued, "Word is a message was received this month from Japanese leaders that they're willing to negotiate a peace but not willing to accept unconditional surrender."

"It'll never work. I understand our people have issued an ultimatum calling for unconditional surrender, including plans to occupy Japan, disarm the country and bring their war criminals to trial."

It was only after Japan ignored the ultimatum that the United States decided on an alternative to an invasion of Japan, which they knew would cost countless lives on both sides. On August 6 the Enola Gay, a B-29 bomber, dropped an atomic bomb on Hiroshima. Three days later another atomic bomb was dropped on Nagasaki. Thousands of Japanese were killed and wounded. After the second bomb Japanese leaders realized they were helpless against such power.

On September 2, 1945 aboard the battleship *Missouri* in Tokyo Bay the Allies and Japan signed the surrender agreement. V-J Day came three years, eight months and twenty-two days after Japan bombed Pearl Harbor in Hawaii.

~ ~ ~

June 29, 1950

Dear Mary,

Congratulations on receiving that grant. Your folks must be very proud of you. How long will you be studying in New England? Getting the chance to go with members of the art department faculty is a real feather in your cap. Your painting must be great. Hope I get to see some of your work some day.

Isn't it strange how we keep missing each other. I haven't been home very often but the few times I've been there, you've either just gone on an art trip or are visiting friends or relatives somewhere else. Ships that pass in the night and all that.

I worked in both Zion and Bryce Canyon National Parks but wanted to be out in the wilderness farther, away from so many people so I finally got transferred here to Mt. Rainier National Park in Washington state. The mountains are beautiful and green. I just hope the park doesn't become too much of a tourist attraction. Already I'm seeing more hikers and campers than last year.

My address will be the same for the time being. Send me your new address as soon as you get settled. Some day we're sure to come face to face.

My best,
Rick

~ ~ ~

"I can't believe you're really here!"

"Well I am. In the flesh. Where are those beautiful twins I've heard so much about?"

Emma led Mary to the family room where three-year-old Nicco and Becky were happily piling blocks on top of each other then knocking them down.

"Nicco?"

"Nicholas for Nick Grosso, you remember him. He and Jerry were in Italy together, and James for Jerry's uncle."

"And I can guess why Becky."

"Right. Rebecca for our wonderful teacher and Olivia for my mother."

As they sat and watched the children play, Mary's expression was tinged with nostalgia, "It's times like these I wonder if I've made the right choice."

"You mean about marriage."

"Yes."

"You're not that old, you know. Have you found someone?"

"The jury is still out on that."

"Then you've made the right choice. Marriage is great if everything is right." Emma grimaced, "I hate to think what marriage to the wrong man is like."

"How *are* Connie and Max doing?"

"I've only seen Connie twice since we moved to Salt Lake. They've moved to Sommerset but from what I hear Max is a real jerk as a husband and father. Connie's holding down two day jobs now with the kids in school all day. She worked nights before. Apparently Max doesn't contribute anything but trouble. She looks tired but never says a word against him."

"That's too bad," Mary said. "I hear Robbie's not doing a great job, either."

"He's not. He's got a serious drinking problem but Ivy acts like everything is wonderful. She always was able to blot out things she didn't want to acknowledge. And it appears Robbie has the same ability."

"Who would've dreamed those two guys would turn out like they did. Max always was a bully but I thought he'd outgrow it when he went into the army. And Robbie seemed like such a nice kid when we were growing up."

"He was. I can't say I'm too surprised about Max but I did think Robbie had a lot going for him. But enough of them. Tell me what's happening in your life."

"I've got some news I've been dying to tell you." Mary smiled, "Remember that Easter picnic when we climbed the mountain and talked about wanting to see more of the world than Grassville?"

"Yes. And I still do. Why?"

"I'm going to Europe next month to study with some of the great painters there."

"That's fantastic! I am so happy for you." Emma glanced at the children, "And if it weren't for these two, I'd be envious! How long will you be there?"

"Three or four years. I'll spend the first year in France, mostly Paris but some other places, too. Then I'll go to Italy and Germany, then spend the last year in Spain, home of my ancestors."

"That's absolutely wonderful! Everything I read says Europe is moving along nicely with reconstruction since the war." Emma sighed, "How I wish I could spend some time over there with you."

"Why don't you plan to come over for a couple of weeks in a year or two. I'm pretty sure I'll know my way around by then."

It was Emma's turn to grin. "I'm afraid I'll be too busy in a year or two." She patted her stomach, "I'm expecting again."

"Now I'm the one who's almost envious. That is so great!"

"Yes, we're delighted. Jerry and I have always wanted at least four kids so if all goes well our traveling will have to come later. But we have agreed that when the time is right we're going to travel. We both want to visit Great Britain and Ireland as well as Scandinavia and Europe and Greece. And that's just for starters."

"Looks like you've got it all planned out."

Emma laughed, "You know me. I always did like to plan ahead. That's never changed."

Mary chuckled, "I'm glad. I hope you never change."

"Likewise. Be sure and write and tell me all about the places you see. I love your illustrated letters. And now you'll be able to add scenes to help keep my dreams alive."

~ ~ ~

"So, Mary Ruiz, after all these years we finally meet face to face."

"I'm just sorry it's at such a sad time, Rick."

"Don't be sorry. They both lived full lives. And it's not a sad time for them. They're finally together again. After mom died, dad tried to hide it but I knew he was just marking time until he could join her."

Rick was even more handsome than his photos and Mary was more delicate and beautiful than hers. Their letters to each other the past twenty years had increased in numbers and intensity until they knew each other intimately. They gazed at each other oblivious of the people around them.

* * *

"How is that lovely daughter of yours?"

Rick grinned proudly, "M 'n M is doing great. She got a giant head start on us and has two and a half kids already. She told us when she was very young that she wasn't going to wait until she got old to get married and have kids."

Mary laughed, "And she kept her word. She was a very determined girl almost from the minute she was born."

M 'n M had been a miracle baby. Rick and Mary were told they would be unable to have children but two years after they married Mary discovered she was pregnant. The doctor told them to expect a severely retarded child if they didn't end the pregnancy but Mary's mother, Maria, assured them the baby would be fine.

They still worried until the night Mary dreamed Rick's mother, Molly, came to them and repeated the same words Maria had said. When she told this dream to Rick he nodded and said, "That sounds just like ma. What do you want to do?"

Mary replied, "I can't explain it but I feel at peace, like we're going to be okay."

And so Molly Maria was born, whole, bright and filled with determination and vitality. She talked early, walked early and had well-formed opinions by the time she was three years old. She was a delight and blessing to her parents and her Ruiz grandparents.

"I wish your parents could have known her," Mary said quietly as they watched her take her first step.

Rick put his arm around Mary and replied surely, "Oh, they know her all right. I'm convinced they've known her longer than we have."

~ ~ ~

"Are you staying here in Sommerset tonight?"

"Yes," Jerry said, "we didn't want the stress of driving all the way back to Salt Lake after the reunion. What about you?"

"We're staying here, too. We sold my old home in Grassville. We hung onto it for sentimental reasons for a few years after dad died but when we realized the drive from Taos was too hectic with a lively baby we decided to sell. But we're going to drive up to Grassville tomorrow for a visit with Selena. Why don't you two come with us."

Emma and Jerry looked at each other. She had tried to hide her weariness but Jerry saw it in the slump of her shoulders. He also saw the gleam in her eyes. "What a good idea. Jerry, let's do it."

Whatever she wanted. He knew better than to try to change her mind once it was made up. "Okay, if you feel up to it who am I to argue." He turned to Rick and Mary, "What time are you leaving?"

"When we get up," they said in unison. Sleeping in didn't come as easy as it once did.

Rick added, "Just knock on our door when you're ready."

Chapter Six

They danced slowly to the medley of familiar old favorites. As the orchestra moved from *It's Been a Long, Long Time* to *Unforgettable* to *Love Letters,* Jerry held Emma close savoring the faint fragrance of her hair and the ease with which she followed his every move. He softly hummed along as the music shifted to *Autumn Leaves* and they both quietly sang the words to *September Song.*

"Those words are right," Emma murmured as the music drew to a close, "the days *are* dwindling down to a precious few."

Jerry nodded, unable to speak. His emotions were too close to the surface. She recognized the tensing of his muscles and glanced around hoping to find something to divert his attention.

"Look. Over there by the bandstand. Is that Stefan and Sophie? I can't see their faces clearly."

"You're right, it is. Should we work our way over and say hello?"

"Why not. It's been ages since we saw them last."

As they moved slowly around the perimeter of the dance floor the rumors that had spread about Sophie when Stefan was off to war flashed into Emma's mind. Knowing what her mother thought of gossip, she hadn't asked her much about Sophie on her visits home from college.

But Ivy hadn't been reticent about the questions surrounding their former classmate's fiancee, Sophie Peters, and her disappearance from Grassville the spring the war ended. "Sure, she's engaged to Stefan but that doesn't stop her from flirting with other guys. Mom says she's no better than she ought to be and I agree with her."

Emma clamped her mouth shut so she wouldn't respond with a retort about how fast the time had gone since the same rumors were flying about Daisy. "But you don't really know for sure, do you?"

"What's to know? Why else would she skip out two months before graduation?"

The rumors quieted when Sophie returned to town that same August, alone. But unanswered questions still hovered.

"What difference does it make?" Olivia had said to her daughter before Emma returned to B.Y.U. in the fall. "You'd be wise to pay less attention to Ivy and more attention to important issues, like how soon all our boys will be able to return home."

And Emma had agreed, she remembered, as they reached Stefan and Sophie Louganis.

"It's good to see you two again. How are you?"

Stefan smiled that dazzling smile they remembered so well, "Great! What about you two?"

A shadow flickered across Jerry's eyes so swiftly Stefan wondered if he imagined it.

Emma spoke quickly, "We're in great shape...for the shape we're in." They laughed at the old saw. She continued, "Tell us what's been happening since we saw you last."

"Stefan's planning to retire in a couple of years," Sophie replied as she looked at him tenderly. "After that we plan to do some serious traveling."

"You took over your dad's practice in Grassville after he retired, didn't you?"

"Yes," Stefan laughed. "During the war when I was a medic and working frantically to patch up our guys I vowed never to join the medical profession. But after we got married," he slipped his arm around Sophie's waist, "I realized I not only wanted to be a doctor like my dad, I wanted to work with him."

"What about your family?" Emma asked. "You've got two kids, if I remember correctly." She was surprised at the minute flicker that crossed Sophie's face. "Are they in Grassville, too?"

Stefan spoke up proudly, "Steve is a doctor in Denver. He and Bonnie have three kids, all attending Colorado State in Fort Collins. 'Thena and Mark live here in Sommerset. Their three oldest kids go to B.Y.U. Stephanie, their youngest will be a senior here when school starts."

"We're really proud of all of them," Sophie added, her smile not quite reaching her eyes.

* * *

"Go ahead, silly, give her a call."

"What if she says no?"

"You won't know any less than you know now. And it'll be one more name to cross off your list."

Alan hesitated then picked up the phone. Lisa was right. The last two calls had been dead ends. He couldn't be farther behind than he was already.

~ ~ ~

Sophie heard the phone ringing as she tried to unlock the door. But it stopped before she got to it. Just what I need, she thought, one more person asking me to work on another committee.

She was frazzled. Steve and 'Thena would be home from school in less than an hour and, if things went as usual, they would both need the car, so she would be stuck driving them again. And, undoubtedly, they'd be heading in opposite directions like always.

She hadn't even thought what to cook for dinner and Stefan would need to eat the minute he got home before heading out for visits to the homebound.

How did life get to be so hectic? Thank heavens they'd stopped after two kids. She'd go crazy if she had any more to worry about. That thought gave her pause.

~ ~ ~

"What about it, honey? Can you get away long enough to go to the convention in Salt Lake with me next week?"

Sophie gazed at Stefan's eager face. It had always glowed with love for her. Love she felt unworthy of. She frowned.

"Don't worry about it," he said. "I just thought it would be great to get away, just the two of us, for a couple of days. But I know how much you worry about the kids." He turned away, the disappointment clear in his voice, "It's okay."

"No," she hurried before he left the room, "I do want to go with you. I know the kids'll be okay."

His smile was dazzling. The same smile that made her fall in love with him. The same smile that lit up his face whenever she walked into a room. The same smile that haunted her years earlier when she had made the hardest decision she had ever made.

~ ~ ~

"No, I don't want to see it! I don't want to know what it is! I already signed the papers. Don't say any more!"

"But Miss Peters, are you sure you really want to give h...it up?"

"Yes, I'm sure. Don't ask me again. Just hand me my clothes so I can leave."

"Oh, you can't do that."

"Just watch me!"

"But it's midnight. The doctor hasn't signed your release forms."

"Go call him. I've gotta get out of here."

While the nurse hurried away to phone Dr. Wallace, Sophie threw off the hospital gown and grabbed for her clothes, buttoning buttons and zipping zippers as she crept down the deserted hall. She didn't wait for the elevator but pushed through the heavy door to the stairs and rushed down them, pain and dizziness making her steps falter.

She opened the door on the first floor and peeked out. The dimly-lit lobby was empty. She held onto the wall as she made her way to the main door feeling the warm moisture between her legs.

She waved down a cruising taxi and gave him the address of the cheap motel she had been calling home for the past few months. She had enough money to stay here two more nights and buy her bus ticket home. Her mother had given her every cent she had. They had made up a story that Sophie was needed to help a sick cousin for her dad, knowing he would be furious if he knew the truth. His temper was legendary.

Tomorrow was the first day of August. She should be well enough to travel and be home before the week was out. Had her mother been able to keep her dad in the dark? She knew her name would be bandied about around town but that didn't matter as long as the truth could be kept from Stefan and her dad.

Sophie was a good student so her teachers had agreed to let her take her books with her to complete her school work. She had spent her days in Boise during April and May between her motel room and the public library.

She knew her mother had gone to Sommerset and picked up her diploma and had it waiting for her at home. She wished she had been able to participate in the graduation exercises. I was so stupid, she thought again, so miserably stupid!

She had loved Stefan for as long as she could remember. And when that love was returned she thought all her dreams had come true. She fully intended to stay true to him while he was gone to war but when a group of friends suggested going to the Harvest Ball in Sommerset, Sophie had agreed. It had been hard sitting on the sidelines while her friends danced so when that handsome serviceman who was home on leave asked her to dance she couldn't resist.

And before she realized what was happening they were in the back seat of his car while her friends continued to dance inside. No one had seen her leave and no one saw her return to the ballroom. She was sure no real harm had been done. She had been dead wrong.

And the worst of it was that there had been no love involved, just desire and exigency. Everything happened so fast she didn't even know his name. She never saw him again.

~ ~ ~

"Ya sou, pehdi mou, ti kanis?"

Sophie glanced up in surprise. Stefan's grandmother was in the flower garden just inside the fence. She hadn't seen her there bending over, pruning the roses.

"Poli kala, kiria," she smiled, "kyesis?"

"Ah, Sophia," she always used the Greek pronunciation, "you learn Greek for my Stefan, yes?"

"I'm trying," the young woman answered, "but I'm not learning it very fast."

"You do good. Very harda learn new language. When I come to 'merica I no spikka da English. After alla dis time still harda 'member alla word."

"Well, you certainly know more English than I do Greek. You should be very proud of yourself."

"You good girl. Come, we sit an' talk."

The two walked over to a bench under a large maple tree at the corner of the house.

"You no looka happy. You missa Stefan?"

Sophie nodded, the tears close, "I miss him so much."

"I know." Then, in her broken English she told Sophie how she had waited seven years in her little village in Greece for her husband to earn enough money to send for her. "My Stephano work in coal mine all over Carbon County. When I come we live ina Castle Gate."

Goldie Louganis told how terrible it was when her dear Stephano was one of the 172 miners killed in the terrible mine disaster there in 1924. That was when her son, Steve, and his wife, Athena, insisted she come to Grassville to live with them.

"You no worry. My Stefan missa you, too, an' he be home soon." She laughed, "Then we have a bigga wedding party."

Oh, I hope so, Sophie thought, I hope so.

~ ~ ~

"I am so glad you're home, mom. I love Grandma Peters but I don't think I could have taken one more day of her soup."

Sophie hugged her son and laughed, "I know, honey. I remember getting awfully tired of soup when I was a kid."

"By the way, you got a phone call yesterday."

"Who was it?"

"I don't know. He wouldn't give his name."

"Did he say what he wanted?"

"Naw. Just asked for you. When I asked if he wanted to leave a message he hung up."

Probably somebody needing another volunteer, Sophie thought. I'm too busy already. Am glad I wasn't home.

~ ~ ~

"How many names have you called now?"

"Four," Alan answered dejectedly. He had come up empty every time.

"Can you let it go?" Lisa asked quietly.

He shook his head. "I know there's probably no chance in hell I'll ever know. There's so little information to go on. But it never stops bugging me." He gazed at his wife, envy in his voice, "You are so lucky to know who you are."

"I know who you are, too. You're wonderful and kind and compassionate," she grinned, "and handsome. Just like Robert Redford, only taller. And your eyes are bluer than Paul Newman's."

"Flattery will get you everywhere." But the wistfulness never left his eyes. He sighed, "I wish it wasn't so important to me but I need to know who my parents are."

"You know who your parents are," she said quietly.

Alan thought of Annie and Simon Peterson who had raised him as their own. They had loved him unconditionally, even during his wild teenage years, never giving up on him.

They had been to his every performance, his every game, his every award-winning ceremony. No child could ever ask for better parents.

They had been open about his adoption when they felt he was old enough to handle it. And when he came back from his stint in Vietnam they had worked with him willingly to try and find his birth mother. Without their help he wouldn't have the womens' names he was now holding in his hand.

"Yeah, I do know who my parents are. I just wish I knew why I was given away."

Lisa embraced him. "Okay, then we keep going. How many names are left?"

"Two. I've called the one name a few times already but never been able to make contact."

"Well, let's work on the other name for now then you can keep trying on that last one."

~ ~ ~

Sophie wiped her eyes as Steve walked across the stage and smiled at them as the diploma was placed in his hand. He looked so much like his father they could be twins. His smile, like Stefan's, was enchanting, including the whole world in it's radiance.

"How I wish grandma was still here," Stefan whispered to his father and mother sitting next to him. "She would be so proud."

"Oh, I think she's here, her grin as wide as yours," Steve smiled. "Is my namesake still planning on going into medicine?"

"Yes. He got a scholarship to the University of Utah for his undergraduate work then plans to go to Boston to medical school."

"Following in his father's footsteps all the way, I see," Athena said.

"Yeah," Stefan grinned, "and without any prodding from me. I think he looks more to his grandpa for inspiration."

The older man wiped his eyes, "You've done a fine job with your kids."

"They are good kids. But I'll be the first to admit that the credit goes more to Sophie than me. I've been too busy with my work sometimes but she's always been there for them."

"She's a good woman," Athena nodded.

~ ~ ~

"Wake up, sweetheart."

"Huh?"

"Wake up Sophie. You're having a nightmare again."

Stefan was puzzled. Sophie had always been a light sleeper but hadn't been troubled by nightmares. Until two weeks ago. Her thrashing was frenzied as she moaned and cried, "No, no, no."

As she came to consciousness, Sophie nestled closer to Stefan, glorying in the warmth and safety of his embrace. He was her protector, her lover, her armor against the slings and arrows of the world. He would always be there for her.

Or would he, she thought, as he drifted back to sleep.

Would he still be here for me if he knew the truth? I should have told him years ago.

Why didn't you?

He would have rejected me?

Has he ever rejected you?

No. But he's never had reason to.

Hasn't he?

Sophie wept silently. How easy hindsight was. She wanted desperately to believe Stefan would not reject her. Now she would never know.

If only she hadn't frozen and hung up the phone when the voice on the other end asked her if she was Sophie Peters who had had a baby in Boise in 1945. If only she had not gone to that dance. If only she had been honest with Stefan when he first came back from the war.

If only . . .

If only . . .

So many "if onlys." She drifted into fitful sleep.

~ ~ ~

"Do you believe she was telling the truth?"

Alan nodded. "I double checked everything she said. She was a WAC stationed in London in 1945."

"Then the Peters woman in Grassville is the only one left, isn't she?"

"Yeah. Her name is Louganis now. She's the one I was talking to when we got disconnected."

Lisa wanted to ask if it was possible it wasn't a disconnect, if she had hung up on him. But she didn't have the heart to burst the last ray of hope he had left. He had become obsessed with finding his birth mother. Would he never rest until he got to the bottom of it?

"Are you going to try her again?"

"Later. I'm going to do a little more digging first. If she's not the one then there'll be no one left to look for."

~ ~ ~

There had been no more calls. Maybe she was home safe. Maybe he wouldn't try any more. What could have happened? They promised her the records would never be unsealed. She had made them repeat it twice to make sure she understood.

She had asked about abortion when she first told her mother. "No, Sophie, don't even think about it. I've heard too many stories about women bleeding to death or dying of infections."

May Peters clasped her daughter's hand tightly, "You have to go away...far enough where there's no chance someone we know will run into you. And big enough where you'll be just another face in the crowd."

"How?" Sophie wept. "I don't have any money to go away."

"I've got a little saved. Been putting it away for years. Your dad doesn't know about it." She went to the flour bin and reached her hand carefully behind it. "He'd never think to look here."

She came back to the table holding a tarnished, dented can that had once been filled with lard. It was stuffed with money. She laid the bills on the kitchen table, smoothing them carefully as she piled the bills on top of each other.

In spite of her despair, Sophie was fascinated. She had never seen so much money in her life. "How did you get all this?"

The determined expression on May's face hardened, "I knew if anything happened to your dad there'd be no money to take care of you kids. He means well but I knew if I put it in the bank he'd claim it. So I saved a penny here and a dime there and every time I had enough I went to the store and exchanged it for a one-dollar bill.

"When we went to Sommerset I'd sneak into the bank and exchange the ones for tens and twenties. I knew I couldn't do it here in town without your dad hearing about it."

May took a sock out of Sophie's drawer, rolled up the currency and stuffed it down inside. "Pack this in with your things. It should be enough to last you."

~ ~ ~

"Hello?"

"Is this Mrs. Louganis?"

"Who's asking?"

There was a pause. "My name is Alan Peterson. I called you a couple of weeks ago but we got disconnected . . ."

"Mr. Peterson," Sophie interrupted, her voice hard as steel, "I'm not the person you're looking for. Please stop calling here."

The click on the other end sounded like a death knell to Alan. Maybe Lisa's right. Maybe it is time to end this.

"Have you still got those tour brochures?"

"Yes."

Alan grinned crookedly, "Get them, I'm ready to start going though them."

Lisa's smile was ecstatic as she opened the desk drawer and pulled out the brochures. There were only four tours they could afford. "Where do you want to go?"

"You tell me, first. You're the one who's been waiting for me to get my act together and start living again."

"You're sure?"

"I'm sure."

She picked up the brochure telling of the place she most wanted to visit. They had talked of it before he got so caught up in finding his birth mother. "This is within our price range. We fly to London and join the tour group there." She pointed, "See, it's for a week and even includes a cruise of the islands."

Lisa melted into Alan's embrace, happier than she had been for months.

"Sounds wonderful, babe. Let's get busy and make the arrangements. I'm ready to boogie."

~ ~ ~

"This is wonderful, dad. I couldn't ask for a better graduation present."

Stefan smiled, "I just wish we could have gone when my grandma was alive. She always talked about going back to the old country."

"It's too bad grandpa and grandma couldn't come with us," 'Thena interjected as they drove along the narrow winding road.

"We talked about it," Stefan said, "but agreed we couldn't both leave at the same time. One of us has to be there for our patients."

"They've been here, haven't they?" Sophie asked.

"Yes, they came over the year after grandma died. They wanted to visit with her relatives here. But they didn't do as much traveling as we will."

Stefan and Sophie and the children had left for Greece the second week in June. They stayed at the Fenix Hotel near the airport the night they arrived in Athens and rented a car the next day for their drive across the Corinth Canal on their way to Olympia which was near Goldie's little village.

On the way they stopped to see the ruins of the open-air theater at Epidavros, the ruins of Homer's Mycenae, the Grand Lion's Gate and Beehive Tombs of Agememnon and Clytemnestra, taking turns reading from guide books at each stop. They stayed in small hotels or inns and discussed non-stop how a major civilization had reigned in this fascinating country centuries earlier.

They stayed with their Louganis relatives four days, dancing Greek dances with them, enjoying a variety of tasty dishes and walking through the ruins of the original Olympia.

"Oh, yes," explained Stefan's great uncle Stavros, in British-tinged English, "those early Olympians stressed the importance of the body, the soul and the mind.

"And see here," he continued, "these small, scrawny trees with red blossoms are called Judas trees. The story is that Judas hung himself on one after he betrayed Jesus and from that time forward they never grew tall and strong."

On their way back to Athens they visited the ruins at Delphi. "I'm not sure I can make it all the way to the top," Sophie complained, stopping to catch her breath, using her fan to create a small breeze in the hot, humid air.

"Sure you can, mom," laughed 'Thena on her way back down the mountain, "and you'll be glad you did. They're worth it." She took her mother's arm, "I'll help you."

~ ~ ~

"Isn't this incredible!"

Alan smiled at the joy on Lisa's face. "Yes, it is."

They strolled with other tour group members around the main street of Mykonos, wandering in and out of shops and admiring the stark white buildings with their beautifully colored doors and shutters.

Soon it was time to climb into the little boats for the ride back to the ship, *The City of Rhodes.* What the ship lacked in modern conveniences it made up for in the buffets at mealtimes.

The next day the ship docked at Rhodos and the group took a bus to Lindos where they climbed a multitude of steps to the impressive ruins of the Acropolis. When they descended they rode back into Rhodos and explored the Old Town.

"I still can't believe we're really here."

"Me, too," grinned Alan as he glanced at the crowds on the beach.

"Eyes front, sailor," Lisa laughed as they both watched a number of topless young women playing in the water or sunning themselves on the beach.

"Do you think they've been surrounded by nude statues so long they no longer notice whether the body is clothed or not?"

"Probably. Or they didn't descend from Puritan ancestors. Take your pick. It doesn't seem to bother them."

The following morning they visited Knossos on the island of Crete. The tour director told the story of the Minotaur and took the group into the labyrinth underground where she explained, "The Minoans believed their god lived underground and to placate him so he wouldn't cause earthquakes they built everything underground but," she smiled, "apparently their god was irascible because earthquakes did come and destroyed everything. And they haven't stopped, either. They still have earthquakes on Crete."

"It's both fascinating and frightening to walk around under here," whispered Lisa.

"Yeah," Alan said, "let's hope the god isn't restless before we get back above ground today."

Later that same day they waited in line to ride the tender from the ship to the island of Santorini where they had their choice between riding donkeys up more than six hundred steps to the city of Thira or riding the teleferique.

"I think I should have taken the cable car," groaned Lisa as the donkey climbed too close to the edge for her liking.

"And miss the adventure?" laughed Alan. "I haven't had this much fun in a long time."

Thank heavens, Lisa thought as she watched his glowing face. *I'm so glad he's finally unwinding. The last year has been really hard for him.*

The sight from the top was breathtaking. "Don't worry," the director laughed, "there are small earthquakes here from time to time but the last major one, which destroyed most of Thira, was in 1959. I'm pretty sure we'll be fine today."

"Pretty sure?" murmured Lisa, "it'd be nice to have a better guarantee than that."

"Are you sorry you came?"

"Not a bit, sweetie. I just wish we weren't flying home day after tomorrow. I could stay here in these islands forever."

"Somehow I don't think our jobs will wait that long," Alan laughed. "But it has been wonderful. Thank you so much for sticking with me and finding this little bit of heaven."

~ ~ ~

"I've got to pick up something for mom," Sophie said. "Do you want to come into the Plaka District with me or wait here?"

Stefan, Steve and 'Thena answered in unison, "Wait here." They settled on a bench under a tree as Sophie walked down the narrow street trying to avoid eye contact with vendors on either side trying to lure tourists into their shops.

Yes, she thought, as she spied a shop with small marble curios in the window. The vendor was standing inside, smiling, making no effort to lure shoppers inside. All the items displayed looked like better quality than some of the other things she had seen, too.

She wandered around the small space grateful the owner was not trying to push her to buy something. She took her time and finally came upon an exquisite miniature green vase, a perfect fit for her mother's window box.

She felt the presence of other shoppers around her but paid no attention to them. Carrying the small gift in her hand she approached the smiling vendor.

"An excellent choice, madame," he said in perfect English as he wrapped it in tissue and took the correct change from her outstretched hand.

Sophie smiled and turned to walk out the door, colliding with a young man directly behind, his eyes on a young woman choosing something in the far corner.

"I'm so sorry," she said as he turned to look at her. The color drained from her face. She was looking into a mirror image of her younger self.

He, too, was stunned as he reached out to steady her. Her knees had turned to jelly.

Lisa turned from the shelf of souvenirs in time to see Alan reach out to the woman whose back was to her. She stepped quickly toward them.

"Alan, are you okay?" He stood as though in a trance.

"Alan?" Sophie whispered. "Alan?" she repeated.

The words wouldn't come out. He recognized his face, as it would look in a few years, staring back at him.

The vendor had come out from behind the counter. His smile was open and friendly, "Ah, madame, your son buys from me, too."

Sophie's glance back up the street was wild.

Alan turned, too, and saw three people sitting on a bench at the head of the street. He knew the men were father and son. They looked almost like twins.

Then he looked at the girl. She was a mirror image of him at age sixteen. None of the trio were looking in their direction.

By this time Lisa had seen Sophie's face. "Are you Mrs. Louganis?" she asked quietly.

Sophie nodded, her stance that of a deer caught in a car's headlights. "They don't know," she murmured. "They don't know."

Alan finally found his voice, "They won't find out from me." He realized for the first time how traumatic this was for the woman standing before him. His birth mother.

Sophie shook her head numbly unable to understand what he was saying.

"It's okay," he said trying to penetrate the shock in her face. "It's okay. Can you get back up the street by yourself?"

"I'll walk with her," Lisa said as she took Sophie's arm, recognizing the ramifications involved here. "They won't recognize me."

Sophie continued to shake her head. The vendor was busy now with another customer.

"Come on, Mrs. Louganis," Lisa said softly. "It'll be all right. I'll stay with you until you can make it on your own."

"My baby," Sophie whispered, tears streaming down her cheeks. "My baby."

"It's okay," Alan repeated, comprehending what this woman had gone through all these years. He, too, had tears in his eyes. "I understand now. I promise you'll never hear from me again."

With difficulty she straightened her shoulders and looked into his face once again. "I had no choice," she breathed. "I was a senior in high school, engaged to a wonderful man who had gone to war." Color flooded back into her face, "He was a soldier, too. I didn't even know his name."

Alan knew she was talking about his father. "It's okay," he said again. "It's okay. I understand."

And he did. The "why?" had never left his thoughts but now he knew the answer. He watched in silence as Sophie and Lisa made their way slowly up the street.

* * *

"So what will happen to your practice when you retire?"

"Mike will keep it going. He's been with me for a few years, now."

"Mike?" Jerry asked.

"My younger brother," Sophie said.

"Little Mikey?" Emma exclaimed, "Mikey who everybody thought the gypsies kidnapped?"

"The same," Sophie laughed, "only he's not so little now. He's 6' 3" and has shoulders so wide he has a hard time finding lab coats to fit."

"Little Mikey . . ." Emma shook her head in wonder. "I still see him as that little tow-headed kid who liked to wander away."

"Well, he's still a tow-head but not wandering anymore. He and Selena are happily settled just a few doors away from us now."

"Selena?" Emma asked, then answered her own question, "Of course. Now I remember Mary writing that her little sister was marrying Mikey...oops, Mike. But I thought they lived in the San Diego area."

"They did. But when their kids and grandkids all ended up here in Utah they decided to move back to be nearer to them."

"Makes sense," Jerry smiled. "Maybe we'll see them tomorrow."

"Are you going up to Grassville?"

"Yes. We're going with Mary and Rick. Will we see you there?"

"No," Stefan answered, "we're staying here with 'Thena and Mark for a couple of days." He shook his head sadly, "I'm going to see if there's anything I can do to help Robbie."

"That's good of you, but what can you do to help?"

"He's come to me for help a few times. I'm going to see if I can talk some sense into him."

"Good luck," Emma said soberly. "You always were his best friend. I hope you can help him."

Jerry took Emma's hand. "What do you say, sweetheart, are you ready to leave?"

"Yes," she replied, the weariness clear in her voice. "It was good to see you two. Stop in whenever you come to Salt Lake."

Stefan's knowing eyes watched as they left the dance. He had a pretty good idea what was happening. He took Sophie into his arms and said, "Shall we swing around the floor some more before we head out?"

"Yes, I'd love to." She smiled and added softly, "And I love you."

Chapter Seven

The two couples stood at the foot of Rebecca's grave. They had brought flowers to put on it. The grave was well-tended. They knew the townspeople had told the story of this wonderful teacher to each new generation.

"I wish I had known her." Rick said quietly as the others wiped their eyes.

"You would have loved her," Mary said.

"As we did," added Emma.

"She affected so many lives," Jerry said, "even the worst kid in town was changed by her."

"Josh Forrester," Mary and Emma said in unison.

"Josh Forrester?"

"He was the worst rag-tag, troublemaker ever."

Emma explained, "His dad skipped out right after Josh's sister was born. He was only three. His mother took in washing and ironing and turned her house into a boarding house. She and the kids slept on the floor in the kitchen and she let out the other rooms. Every morning the three of them got up early and folded up their bedding before the boarders came in for breakfast."

"He must have been very angry," Rick said.

Emma grimaced, "Even his mother couldn't handle him. He beat up every boy and terrorized every girl in every grade in elementary school.

"Mama and Jerry's aunt helped his mother out whenever they could but he rejected everything they tried to do for him. After he called them every foul name he could think of they couldn't take any more and stopped trying."

"Josh wasn't even in Rebecca's class but when she learned he had been passed from grade to grade without ever learning to read," Mary said, "she set out to help him."

"We didn't find out until after she died how much she had done for him. He told us then that she had spent time with him before and after school until he learned to read. In the process he also learned how to behave."

"How did she accomplish what no one else had been able to?"

"He didn't say. We assumed he was attracted first by her beauty and after that realized she wasn't sitting in judgement but simply wanted to help him."

"What happened to him after that?"

Jerry smiled, "He dropped out of school when the war started and joined the army. He lied about his age and forged his mother's signature to get in."

He went on to tell how Josh had been with the 60,000 prisoners who were captured on Bataan.

"Yes," Rick said, "when we heard about the 10,000 prisoners who died of starvation and maltreatment during the Bataan Death March it strengthened our resolve to win the war. Did he make it home?"

"Yes." Emma added ruefully, "I'm afraid I was naive and obtuse in those days. I asked him if he had been tortured."

"Did he answer?"

"He did. Very patiently and with a look of unutterable sadness he lightly said he had been hung by his thumbs more than once.

"But he said something else I've never forgotten. The prisoners had nothing with which to take care of themselves. He said he saved his teeth by taking strands of his own hair and twisting them together to clean his teeth. Like we use dental floss now."

"What happened to him after the war?"

"He stayed on as a career soldier. He rose to the rank of colonel before he retired."

"Does he live here in Grassville?"

"I don't know. The last time we saw him was at Fort Douglas," she glanced at Jerry, "do you remember why we were there?"

He shook his head.

"He introduced us to his seventeen-year-old daughter, a real beauty." She paused. "I wonder whatever's become of them."

* * *

"Why are you doing this?"

Jenny looked at her father solemnly, "Because it needs to be done."

He shook his head. After all he had been through he couldn't possibly understand her actions.

She saw the pain cross his face, "Come on, dad, it's not the same thing you went through."

"Men are caged over there just like I was. That's not different."

"That's one of the reasons I joined the protest movement. Nixon just keeps sending more men like they're expendable."

In all honesty, Josh couldn't disagree. He had been a military man long enough to know you don't go into battle without a clear plan. And the longer the Vietnam war, or police action as it was being called, continued the more tangled the reasons for getting involved became.

Like the rest of the country, he had believed in the domino theory at first. But, as time went on, it became obvious that was the excuse the Johnson administration had used to involve the U.S. in Vietnam.

When Nixon was elected president and announced the first of several withdrawals of U.S. forces in June, 1969, Josh hoped the Vietnamization policy would work. But many Americans were still not satisfied.

His beautiful college daughter joined the Moratorium Day demonstrations for peace on October 15, 1969. One month later she was with the 300,000 antiwar protesters in Washington D.C.

Josh was hurt by her actions but accepted her right to fight for what she believed. He saw much of his younger self in Jenny.

But the following April when U.S. and South Vietnamese troops invaded Cambodia to attack North Vietnamese supply depots, even Josh felt Nixon was widening the war.

"Nixon claims it will save the lives of American troops in South Vietnam and shorten the war," Jenny said in disgust.

Josh could only shake his head. The war was already the longest war in which the U.S. had ever been involved. He supported the men under his command and the troops in Vietnam with all his heart but was dismayed at the actions being taken by his Commander in Chief and his advisers.

More U.S. planes were shot down. More American servicemen were captured and held prisoner. More stories were surfacing about the atrocities committed against them.

The war continued three more years after Josh retired from the service. As he watched newly released American prisoners of war finally boarding planes to come home, Josh quietly wept...for the POWs, for the returning troops being harangued by citizens of this country which meant so much to him, and for those missing in action whose fate would never be known.

"Dad," Jenny said quietly, "I want you to know I never condemned or vilified our men. My fight was with the politicians who used them so cruelly."

"I know, my dear, and I appreciate that." Josh put his arms around her. "I wish the whole debacle had never happened. I wish we could live together in peace without putting each other in jeopardy." He shook his head, "But I've lived long enough to realize that that will probably never happen. I only hope your future children will never have to be put in harm's way."

* * *

As they turned from the grave to leave the cemetery they watched as a white-haired man holding the hand of a young child entered the gate. The man held himself stiffly erect yet unfolded with ease as the child spoke to him.

Their voices carried across the clear morning air. "Yes Sammy. We are going to put these flowers on grandma's grave. Then I'm going to take you over and show you where a dear friend of mine is buried."

"Did he die in the war?"

He smiled gently, "It's not a man. Do you remember me telling you about a teacher I had who saved my life?"

"Yes."

"Well, it's her grave I'm going to show you."

As he said this he glanced in the direction of her grave and saw the four people coming from it. He stopped in amazement. "Is that you, Emma?"

"In person," she laughed, "You remember Mary and Jerry, don't you?" she added as she indicated each of them.

He smiled in delight as he shook their hands.

"And this is my husband, Rick Kenner," Mary said.

As the men shook hands Rick said, "I've heard a lot about you, Colonel Forrester."

Josh's laugh was filled with mirth, "I'll just bet you have." He added, "And I'm afraid most of it is true. I was quite the rascal growing up here."

"Actually," Rick smiled, "I did hear some of that. But it seems the rest of your life has certainly outweighed those years."

"I hope so." He turned to Emma, "How long are you here for?"

"We'll leave for Salt Lake this afternoon."

"Why don't you stop at my place before you leave town. I'm next to the church. Jenny and her children are here visiting with me." He smiled at the child holding his hand, "Samuel here is her youngest."

Emma looked at Jerry. "Whatever you want," he said.

"We're going to stop in and see Joe now, then Mary's sister has invited us for lunch. We should be to your place around one-thirty or so."

"Good. I'll be looking forward to you."

~ ~ ~

"Come in! Come in! When Billy told me you might stop in to see me I kept my fingers crossed you'd make it."

As they stepped inside, Jerry looked closely at Joe's haggard face. The lines of stress and pain were more than just missing Sally. Jerry had seen enough the past few months to recognize a condition deeper than loneliness.

Joe showed them into his light, airy living room and indicated chairs for them to sit in. As they sat, Billy and Sylvia stepped in and joined them. "Glad you could make it."

Rick and Joe clasped hands, gratitude written on Rick's face. "Thanks for all you did for my dad."

"It was my pleasure," Joe said solemnly, "he was a good man and was always more than fair to me. Your ma, too." He glanced at his brother, "You remember how many times she brought supper over for us, don't you, Billy?"

"She sure did. And she was a great cook, too." He grinned playfully at his big brother, "She knew how to add spice and variety to everything she cooked."

Joe laughed, "A little different than the meat and potatoes I always cooked wasn't it."

"How is the mill doing now with young Grosso running things?"

"Isn't it strange how young people become when they're just a few years younger than us," Emma laughed.

Nick's younger brother, Roberto, had gone to work at the mill after the war. He rose fast and became Joe's assistant long before Joe had to finally admit the job took more strength than he had.

"Bob's doin' a great job. I knew right from the first he'd be good. Your dad knew it, too. He told me more than once to keep an eye on young Grosso, he was a comer."

"Your home is beautiful," Mary said as she gazed at the soft colors and patterns. She did a double take at the painting hanging above the fireplace. She stood and walked toward it.

Joe smiled, "Yeah, it's yours."

Mary was stunned. "Where did you get it?" She recognized it from a group she had done for a show nearly fifteen years earlier.

"Billy bought it for me. He knew how much I wanted one of your pictures so he bought it for my birthday."

Emma walked over and studied it. "It's the one of the mountain that Easter, isn't it?"

Mary smiled, "I told you that day is imprinted on my mind."

Jerry studied it and smiled, too. "I don't think any of us will forget that day."

The others looked puzzled but the three didn't volunteer any more information.

"Will you have lunch with us?" Sylvia asked.

"Thanks. Selena's already invited us for lunch." Emma looked at her watch, "She'll be expecting us soon."

"Would you like the grand tour before you leave?"

"I'd love it," Emma answered. "Joe showed us around when they got married but it looks like you've done some remodeling."

"I'll stay here with Joe," Jerry said as the others walked out of the room.

"I know what's on your mind," Joe grinned, "and, yes, it looks like Emma and me are on the same team again...it's too bad it's not tennis like the old days."

"Are you taking anything?"

Joe grimaced, "I did when it first happened. But not this time around. What about Emma?"

"She says there's no point since each medication she's had to take the past few years to control the disease has contributed to the problem now. She calls it the battle of the toxins." Jerry continued quietly, "And I can't disagree with her. When she first learned about the medications she would need to pull the counts down I kidded her about having the choice between being shot and being hung. She agreed."

"Yeah," Joe said. "When I was first diagnosed they made all kinds of promises about the wonders of modern medicine, so I did whatever they recommended. But when it come back I decided it wasn't worth goin' through again. They really can't guarantee nothin'. I know that and they do, too. Has she said anythin' to Mary or your kids?"

"No, she wanted to put it behind her this weekend. I don't know whether or not she's decided to write to Mary about it later. But she has agreed to talk to the kids soon. What about Bill and Sylvia? Have you said anything to them?"

"Naw. I figured we just as well enjoy this visit while we can. I'll write to 'em after they go back. I'm like Em, eventually I'll tell 'em, but not yet."

Jerry walked over to a desk in the corner and picked up a model of a half-finished Spanish galleon. The detail was meticulous. "This is incredible."

"Thanks, it gives me somethin' to do when I can't sleep at night. I've always been fascinated with ships. That's the one thing I wish I coulda done...gone to the ocean."

"I wish you could've, too. It's so massive and powerful and ceaseless. I can understand why the poets use it so often as a symbol of immortality. Have you ever read John Masefield's *Sea-Fever*?"

"Yeah. Rebecca helped me read and understand it that year she was here."

"I didn't know you were in any of her classes."

Joe laughed, "I wasn't. She used to talk to me sometimes after school." Joe pulled a well-worn picture of a galleon from a drawer near the model, "She gave this to me. She gave me pictures of other ships, too. But this is the one she told me I should build. I been workin' on it for a few years now. I hope I get to finish it."

Jerry nodded as the others came back into the room.

"We'd better head over to Selena's. She expected us ten minutes ago." Emma hugged Joe, "It's so good to see you."

"Thanks for stoppin' by. Take care," Joe called as he watched Emma leave, "we'll meet again."

~ ~ ~

Selena was delighted to see them. "¡Hola Mary! ¿Como estás?"

As the sisters embraced Mary replied, "Bien gracias. ¿Y tu?"

"Just great now that you're finally here." She turned to Rick, "And you? How was the trip for you?"

His smile was wide as he held her hand, "Everything went very well. Your big sister takes good care of me."

"Yes. She took good care of us kids when we were little, too." She led them out onto the back patio. "Sit down while I bring out the food. Mike should be here in a few minutes." Selena looked at Jerry and Emma, "He wants to see you two before you leave."

"What about his patients?"

"He planned to take time off as soon as he heard you were coming." She looked at Jerry, "He still remembers you finding him up on the mountain that time." She laughed, "Or he's heard it so many times it's become his memory whether he really remembers it or not."

"Tengo hambre," a deep voice boomed from the carport, "mangiamo!"

"Wow!" Emma laughed, "Multilingual!"

Selena smiled as she carried food to the table, "He's a showoff is what he is," she said as Mike walked out onto the patio. "He knows a half dozen words in a half dozen languages and uses them whenever he's got an audience."

"Gotta be able to talk to all my patients," Mike grinned.

"Sophie wasn't kidding," Emma chuckled, "you have grown a heap since the last time I saw you."

"All Selena's good home cooking," he grinned as he flexed the muscles beneath his sleeves. "That and clean living."

They laughed as he shook hands all around before sitting at the table with them.

"You'll never guess who came in today."

"Okay. I give up. I'll never guess. Who?"

Mike glanced around the table, "Somebody you all probably remember."

Selena shook her head, "He loves guessing games and puzzles. Humor him."

Emma grinned, "Rosie Grosso? Milt Sorensen? Anabel Livingston? Stan Burgess? Michael Jackson? Al Gore? Jay Leno? Whitney Houston? John Stockton? Ann Landers? . . ."

Mike threw up his hands, "Okay! Okay! I get your point. Daisy Greeley Bond."

"Daisy?"

"The one and only Daisy."

"Is she sick?"

"No, she didn't come as a patient. She wants to rent the upstairs apartment over the office where Stefan's dad and mom used to live."

Emma could hardly believe her ears. "Daisy wants to move back here? I thought she and Mr. Rich-and-Powerful Bond lived in San francisco."

Daisy had met Oliver Bond, cousin to the infamous Sheriff Tony Bond who had killed Rebecca, during the war when he was an officer in the navy. He was building a fortune through shady deals even before the war ended. And Daisy knew about those deals which made him more attractive to her.

They had settled in the Nob Hill district and Oliver had continued to add to his ventures while Daisy wormed her way into the upper echelons of society. They had continued their perilous journey until Oliver was forced to dispose of his holdings and leave California one step ahead of the law.

He pulled strings and threatened important people and was able to keep most of his dealings out of the papers. So it wasn't long until the two were established in Ogden and he began working his deals again. He kept a lower profile this time so most of their former acquaintances knew nothing of the move.

"I heard rumors they left San Francisco some time back but didn't know if they were true." Mike added, "All I know now is that Daisy wants to move into the apartment. She didn't say anything about him."

"Will Stefan let her?"

"Probably. The place has only been used for storage these past years so will need a thorough cleaning. But Daisy said she'll take care of all that if he'll let her have the place."

What in the world could have happened, Emma thought. "Ivy told me last night that Daisy didn't want any part of their dad's estate so she bought her out. But she didn't say anything about her moving here."

"Maybe she doesn't know," Jerry said quietly wondering, too, why Daisy was returning now.

"Is she still as attractive as she was?" Mary asked.

"She looked kinda defeated," Mike said, "but then we're none of us spring chickens anymore."

"Speak for yourself," Selena laughed then pulled a wry face. "Maybe she just got homesick for this sweet little town."

* * *

"Where is that box of scarves? I know I packed them." Daisy continued to mutter as she searched through the shelves in her side of the closet. The box wasn't there.

"Maybe they got mixed up with his stuff." She began pulling boxes off the shelves in Ollie's closet. The boxes contained records of old deals and mergers covering more than forty years. "He ought to get rid of this junk. Some of it might come back and bite him."

But the scarves were not there, either. As she reached to start putting the boxes back she glimpsed a shoe box stuffed back in the corner. She smiled as she remembered when he bought those shoes when they first moved to San Francisco. The shoemaker in that little side street had since gone out of business but Ollie had loved those shoes. Had worn them until they practically fell off his feet.

Surely he hasn't saved them, she thought as she tried to pull the box closer to the front of the shelf. Standing on tiptoe her fingers brushed the corner of the box. But she still couldn't grasp it.

Grabbing her hairbrush she worked the handle to the back of the box and inched it toward her. Didn't feel like shoes. Giving another nudge with the brush she jumped back as the box tumbled to the floor scattering its contents everywhere.

Daisy hurried to pick them all up before Ollie got home. He hated for her to go through his things. She realized it was snapshots she was grabbing and stuffing back in the box. Some were black and white and others were in color. What in the world was he doing keeping photos in an old shoebox?

She glanced at the one in her hand and saw it was an old black and white shot of him in uniform. But who was the child holding his hand? She didn't recognize him.

She reached into the closet where some of the photos had fallen onto his neatly aligned shoes. Wait a minute. Something's wrong here. This one was of a little girl on the sofa in their first apartment, the apartment they had lived in before they moved up on the Hill.

She picked up another photo. This one was of Ollie giving a child a bath. A bubble bath. In their Nob Hill master bathroom.

Daisy sat back on her heels, a feeling of suspicion then horror as she slowly scrutinized more of the pictures.

~ ~ ~

"Here, sweetheart. Here's the ice cream cone I promised you."

"I don't want it now. I want to go home."

"Sure, honey. We'll go home as soon as we finish our ice cream."

"I want to go to my house, not that other place."

"I thought you liked that place."

Shuddering, "Not any more. I want to go home."

"Remember we told your mom we'd be gone for two hours. If we go home now, she won't be there."

"Where is she?"

"Probably shopping. Or maybe she ran away."

"She wouldn't run away and leave me."

"Are you sure? She's left you before. Remember when I found you that time in the park and took you to our special place while we waited for somebody to find her?"

"She didn't leave me. She was hunting all over for me."

"Is that what she told you?"

Lips quivering as tears started. "Yes."

"Well sometimes mamas tell fibs. They have secrets. That's why we have secrets, too."

"I don't want any more secrets. I want to go home."

"Is there a problem here?"

"No officer. We're getting ready to go home. Somebody's tired."

"Are you okay?" He squatted on his haunches as he looked into the child's eyes.

Remember what will happen to your mama and daddy if you tell anybody our secret. "I'm okay. We're going home now."

The policeman rubbed his chin as the two of them got into a dark sedan and drove away. *I've got a bad feeling about this,* he thought as he wrote down the license number and walked over to his patrol car.

"Dixie, I need you to look up a number for me. Call me back as soon as you find out who it's registered to."

~ ~ ~

She recognized none of the children. None of them were over seven or eight years old. Some of the children were dressed and some of them weren't. Ollie was in some of the pictures with them, sometimes only in profile, other times holding them on his lap or lying beside them.

"Dear God," she whispered, realizing it had been over fifty years since she had prayed to him, "what is going on here?"

The doorbell sounded, cutting through her confusion. She pushed the pictures away with revulsion as she rose to her feet and hurried downstairs.

"Mrs. Bond?"

Daisy nodded, unable to speak.

"Is your husband home?"

She shook her head mutely.

"May we come in?"

She moved aside as the police officers stepped into the entry. Forcing herself to move she walked stiffly into the living room and indicated for them to sit down.

"Do you know when he'll be home?"

"No," she whispered before breaking into great, gulping sobs. "I can't believe it. I can't believe it. We've been married for fifty years and I didn't know." She knew she was babbling but couldn't stop, "I've hated my mother for what she made that doctor do to me. For not letting me have more kids. Now I thank God I didn't have kids for him to destroy."

They sat in silence knowing this was not an act. "Destroy how?" Though they were sure they knew the answer.

"Come with me," she said plaintively as she led them up the stairs and into the bedroom where the pictures were still scattered on the floor.

* * *

"We'd better be on our way," Jerry said quietly, "if we're going to stop and see Josh. It's getting late."

"It was so good to see you, Mary."

"You, too, Emma. Will I see you again?" she asked as the two women embraced.

"Absolutely," Emma smiled, "don't know when but we'll definitely see each other again."

~ ~ ~

"Come in, come in. I've been waiting for you." Josh turned to the shadowy forms across the room, "Come and meet some dear friends of mine."

Jenny stepped forward and shook their hands. "Yes, I do remember meeting you years ago at Fort Douglas. I understand you've already met Sammy." She turned as three teenaged girls stepped forward, "And these are my daughters Sarah, Esther and Leah."

"They're up here all the way from Hilldale," Josh said proudly.

Yes, thought Emma. It made sense as soon as she saw the braids and modest, home-made dresses on all the women. "It's good to meet you again. You have beautiful children."

"Thank you. I think so, too. Dad says you all go back a long way together."

Josh grinned, "Longer than you can imagine. We can remember when we got double-decker ice cream cones for a nickel and a pair of shoes for under two dollars."

Emma laughed, "I remember once daddy brought home a pair of shoes my size that I worked like crazy to make fit. Mr. Greeley gave them to him because they were both for the same foot."

"Did you make them fit."

"No. And I was just sick because no matter how hard I tried my foot wouldn't work in the one shoe." She laughed, "I just put another layer of cardboard in my old shoes to keep my feet off the bare ground and waited till we could afford new ones."

Jenny turned to her children, "See, I told you you don't have it as hard as grandpa did."

The children smiled but didn't say a word. They sat quietly and patiently as grandpa and his friends reminisced. They were well-behaved and polite.

"What about some cold lemonade?" Josh asked Jerry and Emma. "Jenny just made it fresh."

"I'd love some," Emma said, looking at Jerry.

"That's an offer I can't refuse."

Jenny nodded to her daughters. They stood and walked silently out of the room.

"Are you staying with your dad long?" Emma asked.

"For awhile," Jenny replied glancing at Josh with such tenderness tears sprang to his eyes. "He's helping me make up my mind. I've always been able to count on him to help me work through tough decisions."

Josh smiled and patted her hand but didn't say a word.

* * *

The young couple twisted their hands nervously as they sat opposite Jenny's parents. They were determined to do what was right but she didn't want to alienate Josh and Martha.

"Are you sure?" Martha asked, trying not to cry.

They nodded. It was a big step but one they had decided after much fasting and prayer. "It's the right thing," Daniel said with certainty.

Josh looked at his daughter, "You know you'll be excommunicated."

"We realize that." Then Jenny's resolve to stay calm burst, "For the life of me I can't understand why we'll be cut off for the exact same thing your grandma and grandpa were exhorted to do! It doesn't make sense for us to be persecuted for the very thing the state's founders proclaimed was the celestial order of marriage!"

"The Manifesto made it different."

She shook her head impatiently, "The Manifesto was given to stop the government from stealing church property and disenfranchising its own citizens."

"The difference is that my grandparents accepted the Manifesto as revelation and agreed to obey it."

Daniel said wryly, "Isn't it strange that the high and mighty in Washington who condemned polygamy as barbaric were the same men who had mistresses and dalliances all across the country."

"Not all of them, I think."

"Maybe not," Jenny said hotly, "but there were plenty who did. And still do. And plural marriage is mentioned throughout the scriptures but no one cries for those pages to be cut out."

Martha was weeping openly by this time. She didn't understand her daughter at all. But, then, she never had. Jenny was always joining this protest or fighting for that cause. She was so convinced she was fighting for the underdog it was often hard to reason with her.

Josh knew what his wife was thinking. They had seen this coming. But he also knew he didn't want to cut off all avenues of communication with their only child.

"We can't give you our blessing," he said quietly "but we do support your right to make your own choices. And we'll always be here if you need us."

~ ~ ~

"Mama never accepted our way of life, did she?"

"She accepted you. And that's the important thing. I wish you could stay longer." He picked up three-year-old Leah as Sarah and Esther held tightly to Jenny's hands. They stood looking at the new grave covered with bouquets and wreaths from yesterday's funeral.

"We can't," Jenny said simply. She didn't add that Daniel was unhappy about them coming at all. He felt it was his patriarchal duty to insist they obey him.

But he hadn't counted on Jenny's fierce determination to be with her father at this time. Daniel had walked away from his own family without a backward glance but Jenny had never severed the ties to her parents.

"Are you happy?" Josh watched his daughter's face cloud over.

"Most of the time." Jenny laughed harshly, "But that's not the point of this life, is it?"

"What is the point?"

"To serve and obey and keep *all* God's commandments. We were never promised a rose garden. Life is full of trials and challenges and hardships. We must hold fast at all times and take what is given to us without complaining."

It sounded stiff and formal and rehearsed. "And what about joy?"

"That will be ours in the worlds to come if we don't falter."

"But the scripture says, 'Man is that he might have joy.'"

"True. But it doesn't mean in this life."

Josh looked at Jenny sadly. Did his sweet daughter really believe life was not to be enjoyed now?

~ ~ ~

"Does Daniel know you're here?" Jenny had not been back to Grassville since her mother's death. But in the years since then she and Josh had written often. He drove to southern Utah when Jenny's baby died. He felt Daniel's resentment of him then but was determined to be with Jenny at that sorrowful time.

He was surprised when Samuel was born. Jenny's health was fragile after Elisabeth's birth. When she died, Josh gently suggested that Jenny wait until she was stronger before having more children. Jenny listened in silence but Daniel proclaimed, "We'll have children when the Lord intends us to!"

"No. When he told me he would need to be gone this week I decided to come and see you." She hesitated, not sure how to explain her dilemma.

She smiled inwardly as she remembered Josh telling her that the best way to get to the point was to get to the point.

The reason Daniel was gone was to make arrangements for Sarah and Esther to marry as sister wives to a leader in a Salt Lake group.

"They're very young. Do they want to?"

"No. They want to finish school and go to college in Cedar City."

"Surely Daniel won't marry them off without their consent."

Jenny's tone was bitter, "He doesn't need their consent. He knows what's best."

"Do you agree?"

She hesitated. She had gone over this in her own mind dozens of times. "Not any more. I did at one time but I'm not so sure now. The girls and I need to be sure before we go any farther."

"What will Daniel do when he finds you gone?"

"He'll be angry and self-righteous and pompous. The years have hardened him. He's sure he's always right."

"Will he harm you or the girls?"

"He won't dare. There's been too much in the news lately about polygamy and the law. He'll storm and fuss and wait for us to come to our senses. At least for now."

Josh held Jenny tight as he had done so many times during her growing years. Whichever way she chose to go he would be there for her.

He thought of the Savior's words, *As I have loved you, love one another.*

"I love you," he whispered to his weeping daughter.

* * *

Josh placed his glass of lemonade on the table in front of the couch as he picked up a magazine and said, "Have you seen this? It came in the mail today."

Emma took the magazine. It had a glossy picture of a beautiful sunset over the Oquirrh Mountains. At the top of the cover were the words:

POETIC JUSTICE
Poems For and By Utahns

She showed it to Jerry. "Becky told us a group she knows were hoping to publish a magazine."

Jerry said, "Good for them. It looks like they did it."

Emma grinned, "She asked if she could send some of my stuff to them. I told her to go ahead but they wouldn't want it."

Josh smiled, "Look at page 7."

Emma opened the magazine. Her mouth fell open in disbelief.

Josh took the magazine from her hands and softly read aloud,

> Crimson-laced sunsets,
> Dapple-streaked trees,
> Staccato rainfall,
> Whispering breeze,
> Snowfall at midday,
> Night-diamond freeze,
> Soft gentle dawn
> night's sorrows appease.
> Snuggling children,
> "Story, grandma, please?"
> Together enjoying
> a shared, tender tease.
> "Ti amo, I love you,"
> Blessed heartsease.

Nothing, niente
is better than these.

"I can't believe they accepted it."

"Why not? It's beautiful," Jenny said quietly.

Josh smiled. "I agree. It talks of all the things I love, too."

"That's nice of you to say that."

"Well, it's true. I've written a few things over the years. Maybe now I'll have the courage to submit some of mine."

"Good idea," said Jerry as he looked at Emma, noting the weariness in her posture and shadows under her eyes. "Are you ready to head home, Em?"

She nodded, rising to her feet. "It's been so good to see you again, Josh. And you, too, Jenny. It's good to meet your beautiful children. Take care of them. Children are so very precious."

"Yes," agreed Jenny, "I know."

Josh walked to the door with Jerry and Emma, understanding warming his face as he shook hands. "Thanks so much for stopping by. I hope we see each other again. Have a safe trip home."

They nodded and walked down the steps to their car.

Chapter Eight

The children were all gone now. They stayed for a week. The house seemed empty without them. Time to put things back in their places and go through items that had been piling up and decide what to save and what to discard.

The photo albums lay out on the table. The kids always liked looking through them. "Is this really you, grandpa?" "Remember when we took that trip?" "Did you really go out in public in those clothes?"

Jerry decided to look through the pages again before putting them back on the shelf. "Look here, Emma, your mother must have taken that the Christmas I got new shoe skates." *I never did tell you I knew it had to be you who told Aunt Emily I wanted them.* "We did have fun skating on the rough ice on the creek, didn't we. I wonder if kids today who skate on the smooth surface of ice rinks have as much fun as we did."

"Look, here's one of us at our wedding reception. Remember how we snuck out early when we got word Robbie and Stefan and Billy were planning to kidnap you for the night?" Jerry laughed, "We had some fun traditions, didn't we?"

Jerry continued to look through the album, stopping to study a picture he had forgotten, watching the children grow, reminiscing about their first home, smiling at remembered trips and special holidays. A wonderful pictorial history of family and friends, good times and difficult times.

He smiled as he looked at the picture of the family in front of their first home in Salt Lake after moving from southern Utah. Becky and Nicco were about the same age

Jerry and Emma had been when they met. It had been a hard move for Becky, he remembered.

Nicco was good at basketball so was accepted quickly by his classmates and the boys at church. Becky wasn't that lucky. She liked to read and write poetry, like her mother, and wasn't interested in boys as the girls she met at school were. Even at church the girls her age were courteous, but aloof. They had their own little cliques and Becky wasn't included in anything outside Ward activities.

Then one of her classmates, Lindy, began making friendly overtures when a teacher used one of Becky's papers as an example of what she expected from the class. When Lindy asked Becky to help her with a book report, she was flattered. Before the report was ready to be handed in Becky realized she was doing most of the work on it. But that was okay because she was finally being accepted. But when it happened a second time, then a third, Becky knew she was being used and refused to continue.

Jerry and Emma knew something was wrong but Becky didn't confide in them or her twin. Nicco and Becky had been close from the beginning. They knew each other's thoughts and often finished sentences for one another. But this time Becky simply grew more quiet.

When Becky wouldn't relent, Lindy turned on her with a vengeance.

* * *

Becky looked warily around the lunchroom. It had been nearly three weeks since her stand-off with Lindy, and she had been subjected to one "accident" after another since then. Someone had trashed her English notebook when she left it on the table in the library to get a book from the stacks.

It had only been a few minutes but when she asked the librarian and a couple of the other students there, no one had noticed anything.

At least once a week, one of Lindy's buddies had bumped into Becky as she hurried down the hall between classes. Each time the girl had said, "Oops, 'scuse me," and sauntered away with a smirk on her face, leaving Becky to scramble to pick up her books and papers before they were trampled on.

Twice she had been shoved roughly from behind when the students were filing into the gym but when Becky turned around all she saw was a mass of giggling classmates talking and laughing with each other, paying no attention to anyone else.

The last incident had happened a couple of days ago when Lindy stood up from her table in the lunchroom just as Becky was passing and "accidently" knocked her tray to the floor. Lindy apologized loudly and profusely, while the gleam in her eyes mocked every word she said.

Becky knew it would do no good to complain. She had no concrete evidence of harassment and to say anything would only make her seem childish.

"How long do you think they're going to keep it up?"

Becky whipped around and saw Margo, with her loaded tray, standing next to her. "What?"

"I said, how long do you think they're going to keep bugging you?" Lifting her feet awkwardly over the bench, Margo sat down without looking directly at Becky and added, "Do you mind if I sit here?"

Do I mind if the biggest nerd in school sits next to me? How could I possibly mind...I'm right there in Nerdville with her. Becky shook her head not trusting herself to speak.

Both girls heard snickering from a nearby table but neither looked up.

"What do you know about them bugging me?"

Margo smiled slightly, keeping her eyes on her tray, "Everybody knows what they're doing. Most kids don't like Lindy but after watching what she and her lap dogs have been doing to you, no one is willing to stand up for you."

"But here you are. Aren't you afraid of them, too?"

"What can they possibly do to me to make my life worse? Everybody already calls me a nerd. Life can't get much worse than that. But it's different for you. You're cute and bright and haven't got a clumsy bone in your body. No wonder Lindy's trying to make you look dumb. She's jealous of you."

"Jealous? You've got to be kidding!"

"You really don't get it, do you?"

"Get what?"

"Lindy barely gets by in school and the only kids who'll have anything to do with her are her three shadows. When you quit hanging around with them, Lindy lost control over you and she doesn't ever like to lose control. That's why they've been giving you such a bad time. Lindy always has been a sore loser."

Becky smiled for the first time in weeks. *Maybe Margo isn't such a nerd. If she shampooed her hair oftener and learned how to style it, she could be kinda cute.*

Perhaps life here in Salt Lake wouldn't be so bad after all.

* * *

"Those were good years, Emma, when the kids were growing up. We were busy all the time but it was a good busy."

Jerry turned another page in the album. Here they all were at Disneyland. And this one was taken at Knott's Berry Farm. "We took some great trips. Remember when we stayed in that motel right on the beach at Laguna Beach? I remember watching you walk on the beach with the water curling around your feet. You couldn't get over the magnitude of it, the constant going out and coming in of the tides."

The memories continued. They were living those years together again.

"Look, here's the picture of Nicco and Roger packing up the car to head down to B.Y.U. Remember when we'd both nearly given up on Roger but Nicco wouldn't quit, wouldn't let him continue to slide down that dead-end road?"

Jerry and Emma had learned about Roger's brush with the law from gossip at church and a small item in the paper.

Roger was the bishop's son, had stopped attending church and started hanging out with a rough crowd.

When they asked Nicco if the rumors were true he told them Roger was basically a good kid but tired of being expected to be the perfect example for all the other young men in the Ward. "It's not only his folks. Everybody else is on his case, too."

* * *

Roger walked slowly. His steps seemed aimless but he knew exactly where he was going; to the place he always went when he needed to think and sort out the messages playing relentlessly through his mind.

This afternoon had been his third visit to the school counselor and the first time he had actually opened his mouth and exposed the tip of his confusion and his jumbled feelings. He hadn't said much but the counselor had looked into his eyes with compassion and waited patiently for him to continue.

But Roger hadn't continued. Once he realized he was sharing a part of himself with the counselor, sharing feelings and thoughts he had never shared with another person, he quickly clamped his mouth shut and said no more.

I can't believe I did that. I can't believe I was so stupid. I knew I shouldn't have gone to him in the first place, but mom and dad were so insistent, so determined that I get help.

~ ~ ~

Matt and Bess Allen were at their wits end. If only there was some way they could help Roger. He had shown such promise as a child, was quick and clever. But now that was all hidden under a sullen cloak of rebelliousness that threatened to drown him, and them with him. If only there was someone to help him. He had refused to see the counselor Matt usually recommended when Ward members needed more help than he could give them.

When they saw Roger at the jail after he was picked up for smoking marijuana, he had seemed like a frightened, lost child. They had known something was wrong for months when they got word he was cutting classes at school.

The judge had actually been very kind. He had made sure Roger understood that if he was picked up again he would be in serious trouble. And the night Roger had spent in jail, though terrifying at the time, had seemed to make him more thoughtful, more willing to follow the rules.

Then they found out Roger was cutting classes again and hanging around with Mac McGowan. Their fears skyrocketed. That's what the argument had been about at breakfast.

"You'll have to hurry so you won't be late for school."

"Nag, nag, nag."

"We have to talk, Roger."

They watched him draw into himself as he had done so many times this last year. Matt opened his mouth to challenge his son then, with sudden insight, realized this was his way of not dealing with things he wanted to avoid. His way of not being drawn into an argument with him.

Bess said gently, "I know we don't have time now, son, but sometime, somehow we've got to sort this out."

"*We* have nothing to sort out," Roger said without looking at them.

Matt sighed, determined not to lose his temper. "I called your school counselor yesterday. He's making time for us during the lunch hour today . . ."

Before he could finish Roger shouted, "You had no right to call him!"

"Yes. As your parents, it was not only our right but our responsibility. We should have done it when we saw things going bad. But we kept thinking it would work itself out. We were wrong.

"When we stood there with you in front of Judge Weston, we realized we hadn't done our job as parents. We've been too busy helping others to realize we were losing our own child."

Roger pushed his chair back from the table with such force it tipped over. He had been planning to skip school and meet Mac. Mac knew where they could pick up some grass.

Damn, he thought as he remembered the judge's eyes when he warned him about staying out of trouble. Without another word, he grabbed his jacket and stormed out of the house.

~ ~ ~

When he got to the stream he worked his way around a clump of trees and mound of boulders on the east bank and hiked carefully to his special hiding place, a niche that had been carved into the bank by a flood years before.

No one knew about this place. Roger had found it when he was still in elementary school and claimed it for his own. He had been careful never to reveal its existence. It was his sanctuary, his haven, his refuge. Whenever he needed to think or plan or plot, this was where he came.

He had nearly shared it with Mac and Theo when they were smoking pot together awhile back. They had just lit up in the old shed on the vacant lot near Theo's when two dogs in the yard across the fence set up such a frenzy they had to flee that hiding place.

They then crept into an empty lot behind a schoolyard but a night watchman's unexpected appearance had nixed that. So they headed toward an empty field at the end of a cul de sac, whispering about where to hang out and smoke. That's when Roger nearly broke down and told them about his secret place. But before he could say anything, a couple of cops showed up and the three of them were handcuffed and taken to jail.

Voices echoed off the banks surrounding Roger. They grew louder, nearer. Although he couldn't make out the words yet, one voice rang with a familiarity he knew too well. He quickly left his sanctuary, walking toward the voices.

"Speak of the devil," Mac grinned, "where you been lately, buddy? Word has it you been goin' to school. That true?"

Roger muttered, "You got it."

"Why? I thought you were through with that crap."

"I thought so too, man, but my folks been on my case like you wouldn't believe."

Roger moved to step past them but Mac grabbed his arm, "What's your hurry?"

"No hurry. Just headin' home."

"Gotta do your homework, schoolboy?"

"Somethin' like that." Once again he started to walk.

"Hold up. I want you to meet my cousin, Rudy."

"He's from Los Angeles," Theo said proudly.

"That so?" Roger tried to sound indifferent as he studied the unsmiling newcomer but failed when his voice cracked.

"Yeah," Mac said arrogantly, "he's here for a couple of weeks. He's been tellin' us about how they do things down there."

Roger nodded, pretty sure where this was heading but not sure he wanted to follow along.

"What about it? You want in on our plans?"

Roger was torn. He was tempted to say yes but something held him back. "I don't know. Let me think about it."

"What's to think about? What's happenin' to you, man? I thought you was one of us."

~ ~ ~

"Hey, Rog, you heading home?"

Roger watched as Nicco pulled alongside him. "Yeah."

"Want a ride?"

"Sure." Roger climbed in beside him.

"Hope you don't mind but I've got to make a couple of stops on the way."

When Nicco turned down a street in a part of town Roger didn't know, he turned in surprise. "What's happening?"

"Got some stuff to deliver." Nicco climbed out of the car and opened the trunk. "Want to give me a hand, here?"

Roger stepped to the back of the car as Nicco handed him a box of groceries. Nicco picked up another box and led the way to the front door of a small stucco bungalow.

"¡Bienvenido Nicco!" The frail woman, holding carefully to her sturdy walker, moved aside as the two boys carried the boxes past her into a small kitchen. The house was threadbare but spotless.

"This is my friend, Roger, Mrs. Martinez," Nicco said.

"Happy to meet you," she smiled.

"Should we put them away?"

"Si, gracias." She sat in a well-worn rocker as the boys put the groceries away, Nicco showing Roger where things went.

As they worked Roger realized that much of the food did not come from a grocery store but looked like food his mother baked and bottled. He turned to Nicco with questions in his eyes but Nicco shook his head, "Later."

As they left the kitchen and stepped toward the front door, Roger noticed a beautiful painting hanging on the wall above a shabby sofa. He walked over to examine it.

"You like?"

The only thing that Roger had cared about lately was creating pictures. He did know about art. "This is a Ruiz, isn't it?" How could she possibly afford it? He'd sell his soul for an original Ruiz.

"Si," she smiled broadly.

Nicco explained, "Mary Ruiz is Mrs. Martinez's niece." He laughed, "She also happens to be a life-long friend of my mother. That's how we met her."

As they drove away Nicco explained that his mother and dad stopped in to visit with Mrs. Martinez often. Emma always checked to see what the older woman needed then proceeded to do her grocery shopping for her.

"Mrs. Martinez is very independent and insists on paying for the things mom buys at the store. But mom always includes things from our garden or pantry knowing Mrs. Martinez will not insult her by offering to pay for these gifts."

"And you don't mind being the delivery boy?"

Nicco laughed, "I like going to her place. She tells some really interesting stories about growing up."

The next stop was at a pre-school for disadvantaged children. Once again Nicco asked Roger to carry in one of the boxes.

"Did some store donate these things?"

"No," Nicco laughed, "we gather up discarded toys and every month one of our Family Home Evenings is spent repairing, mending and painting them."

The Harris family wasn't that much different from his own. "Don't you resent all that 'good works' stuff?"

"Naw. When I see these little kids . . ." Nicco didn't have time to finish before they were surrounded by children calling, "Hey, Toy Man!"

Nicco sat down on the floor and motioned Roger to do the same. The children sat in a semi-circle in front of the young men. Then calling each child by name, Nicco placed a truck or a doll or a stuffed animal into the outstretched hand before him.

Roger was amazed at the joy on each child's face. And was dumbstruck when the child hugged Nicco, then hugged him. The high he got from grass couldn't compare to the high he was feeling now.

* * *

"Yes, Em, I do remember when this was taken." Jerry was looking at a snapshot of the Harris and Phillips families at Lake Powell. The families had pooled their money and rented a houseboat for four days. They explored coves and inlets and spent their nights in sleeping bags, the adults on the boat and the children on the sandstone shore. Sometimes they used the small propane stove in the tiny galley to cook meals but mostly they cooked on the shore using a portable grill they had brought.

He grinned as he recalled playing and swimming in the lake and rubbing lotion on sunburned shoulders. "I remember how that friendship got started, too."

* * *

"Is it true that Sister Phillips is going to get executed?" Six-year-old Tommy's voice was tentative.

"Executed?" Emma asked in surprise. The family was seated around the kitchen table eating Sunday dinner. "What are you talking about?"

Tommy looked confused. "You know...kicked out of the church?"

The whole family had a hard time keeping a straight face. "You mean excommunicated." Emma glanced questioningly at Jerry as she directed her question at Tommy, "Where did you hear such a thing?"

"Danny said his dad told them that was what could happen to their family if any of them did something wrong."

Jerry shook his head sadly. "It's really none of our business," he said quietly. The children recognized the tone in Jerry's voice and didn't pursue the subject. "Tell us what you learned in Sunday School today, Emily?"

Later, when they were alone, Jerry explained to Emma that the rumors were true. "But when it was announced to our quorum this morning we were told not to take the information out of the meeting. I can't imagine what Gene thought he was doing when he took it home to his family."

~ ~ ~

"Dot," Emma said, "I called to see if I can pick you up for Relief Society this morning.

"Yes," Dorothy answered, afraid her voice would break if she said any more. It was nearly a month since the news got out. She had been told she could work her way back into the church if she attended her meetings, she just couldn't participate in all the ordinances. Most of the members tried to be friendly but didn't quite know how to act around her.

But, right from the start, Emma had made her feel comfortable, including her in discussions in which she was involved, acting exactly the same as she always had. It was such a relief from the stiff embarrassment some showed.

As the women headed home after the meeting Dorothy said, "Do you have time to visit for a minute before you go home?"

"Yes. Should we stop off at the drive-in for an ice cream cone first?"

Dorothy nodded. "Do you know why I was cut off?"

"No. And I don't need to know. It's none of my business."

They walked over to a table under one of the maple trees at the side of the building and sat silently enjoying the smooth, rich ice cream.

"You and Jerry have a good relationship, don't you?"

Emma nodded, not wanting to play the role of mother-confessor but knowing Dorothy needed to unburden herself.

"Have you ever felt stifled? Wanted more?"

"Not really. We didn't marry until a few years after Jerry came home from the war so when we did, I was ready."

"Bruce and I got married right out of high school. That's what I thought I wanted at the time. Our first baby was born ten months later. Then, the babies came on a regular basis every eighteen months after that. While I was busy with diapers and feedings and runny noses and scraped knees, he was busy building his business.

"The first year he went to trade school and took plumbing classes. Then he began work for a major company and was called out night and day, sometimes seven days a week. I was content because his wages were growing to support our growing family.

"After a few years he branched out on his own and before long had to hire a helper then another one. The kids hardly ever saw him and the only time we had together was late at night when we were both dead tired. He grabbed an Egg-Macmuffin for breakfast on his way to work and picked up something from a fast food window between jobs for lunch. At first I kept his supper warm for him but it was dried out before he got home so that ended."

The two women sat in silence as they finished the last of their cones. Emma knew Dorothy was asking for neither advice nor absolution.

"When Mark entered first grade it was the first time in all those years I had time to myself. I had no interests or hobbies. The cleaning and cooking moved with rapid precision and took no thought or planning. I found myself with blocks of time with nothing I wanted to do. Watching TV made those empty hours emptier. I was in a rut, bored and boring. Then I met Tyler."

~ ~ ~

Bruce told Dorothy he had hired an accountant to do their taxes. "I need you to meet me at his office to sign some papers."

He was waiting for her beside his truck when she drove into the parking lot and they went into the building together. The interior was decorated richly, plush carpets, polished mahogany furniture and expensive paintings on the walls.

"Ty, this is my wife, Dorothy. Dot this is Tyler Van Winkle." When they shook hands Dorothy felt a frisson of excitement. Tyler was tall and dark with flashing black eyes and a smile to die for. She was glad she had changed out of her usual scruffy pants and tee shirt.

"I'm delighted to meet you, Dot. Bruce here didn't tell me his wife looked like Jane Fonda."

Dorothy blushed as they sat down and Tyler pushed the papers across his desk for them to sign. She knew his words were nothing more than flattery but her hand still tingled from his touch.

~ ~ ~

"Well, Dot, we meet again."

She turned to see Tyler standing beside her table. She had stopped at *C'est La Vie* for a lemonade before heading home after an afternoon of shopping for some new clothes. After meeting Tyler she had taken an inventory of her closet and found everything there was old and out of style.

"Do you mind if join you? I've heard their lemonade is famous."

"Yes...I mean no...I mean of course you can sit down," Dorothy couldn't believe she was stumbling all over herself to find the right words. He must think she was a real airhead. "What brings you downtown?" She flushed. *Now I'm not only an airhead but nosy, too.*

But he didn't seem offended by her question. He smiled his million-dollar smile and said, "I'm taking a long lunch hour. I believe all work and no play makes Ty a dull boy."

She smiled weakly, unsure how to respond.

He glanced at her ZCMI bags. "Do you come here often?"

"Not much." She was too embarrassed to tell him this was her first shopping trip without children hanging onto her. "Are you from Salt Lake?"

"No. I moved here from San Francisco after my marriage fell apart. I've been here less than a year. What about you?"

"I was born and raised here. I've never lived anywhere else." She didn't add that she hadn't traveled anywhere else either.

She looked at her watch. The kids would be home from school in a few minutes. She stood up and pulled out her wallet for money to pay for her drink but Tyler stopped her, "My treat."

"I can't do that."

He grinned roguishly, "I'm not offering to pay for your clothes, just your lemonade."

"Oh...sure...thanks." She turned to leave before he could see her confusion. He was just being friendly. There was nothing wrong with that.

But she found herself thinking of him all the time. The kids didn't pay any attention to her robotic behavior and the only time she and Bruce had together was when they were at church. Even Sunday afternoons never varied. Bruce fell asleep in front of the TV during sports programs and she cleaned up after dinner and tried to keep peace between the children. Her life was still in a rut.

~ ~ ~

The voice behind her in the check-out line was so familiar she wasn't sure if she was fantasizing again.

"So, Dot, I see we both like the same kind of pasta."

She glanced from his cart to hers and started to laugh. The brands of pasta, tomato paste and cheese were exactly the same. "At least you only have to cook for one."

"True. But it gets pretty tiresome eating alone."

"Well, why don't you come for dinner with us some time?" Then she thought of the children and the noise and the clamor. "Then again, maybe not. You'd have to have a cast iron stomach and be deaf in one ear."

Tyler laughed. He seemed to know what she was thinking. "Tell you what. I'll cook lunch for you one day and you can relax and enjoy a meal in peace and quiet."

And, innocent as she intended it to be, that was the beginning.

~ ~ ~

"Bruce has been wonderful. When I told him he forgave me without a second thought, blaming himself for being too busy to see what was happening to us. He went with me to the bishop and we're now going to a marriage counselor."

"I'm glad. You're not the first and you won't be the last."

"Thanks for saying that. You've been so good to me. You listen without judging and don't make unnecessary comments." Dorothy laughed somberly, "I could fill a notebook with all the platitudes I've heard in the past weeks." She paused, "And the worst of it is that I used to mouth those same platitudes myself."

Emma laughed. "We all have at one time or another, not realizing we were doing more harm than good. Basically we're just trying to help each other and don't realize that the help isn't helping. Are you ready to head home now?"

When they pulled up in front of the Phillips house Emma said, "Why don't we take our families up the canyon for a cookout while the weather is still good."

"That would be great. I'll talk to Bruce and see when he's free and give you a call."

The more time the Phillips and Harris families spent together, the closer they grew. Even when the children left home to start their own lives, the two couples continued to share activities and ideas.

* * *

"It was good to see them last night. I just might take them up on their suggestion that we take a trip to Yellowstone Park before winter hits. What about it, Em, wouldn't that bring back old times?"

Jerry closed the photo album and put it on the shelf with the others. It was time now to go through the file and sort out everything there.

"Look here, Emma, remember when you wrote this and I urged you to get it published?" He smiled when he thought of the pleasure on her face when she saw the copy of her first novel in print.

"And here's the folder with all your poetry." He shuffled through the pages. "I didn't realize you'd written so many."

And with that, Jerry knew what he would do to keep her with him until it was time for him to leave. He categorized and sorted until all of them fell into place.

"This one will be the concluding page," he said as he smiled wistfully. "I remember when you wrote this after our Easter holiday with the children and they asked us how we wanted to be remembered."

IN MEMORIAM

"She listened and she loved."
When life's final breath
has passed my lips
and plans are made to lay me
in the ground,
these are the words I hope
will be said of me.

And, in coming years, when
some small glimpse
of me
through melody or memory
drifts across your thoughts,
I would that
"She listened and she loved"
will be the better part
of your remembrance.

And, when time has passed
for you,
and we two once again
smile into each other's eyes,
and love hangs fiercely
in the air between us,
And when all else has turned
to dust
except the sweet yesterdays
we shared,
my dream and hope and wish will be
that you will look at me
and say,
"You listened and you loved."